The Inner House

The Inner House

Walter Besant

MINT EDITIONS

The Inner House was first published in 1888.

This edition published by Mint Editions 2021.

ISBN 9781513281353 | E-ISBN 9781513286372

Published by Mint Editions®

 MINT
EDITIONS
minteditionbooks.com

Publishing Director: Jennifer Newens
Design & Production: Rachel Lopez Metzger
Project Manager: Micaela Clark
Typesetting: Westchester Publishing Services

Contents

Prologue

At the Royal Institution

Professor!" cried the Director, rushing to meet their guest and lecturer as the door was thrown open, and the great man appeared, calm and composed, as if there was nothing more in the wind than an ordinary Scientific Discourse. "You are always welcome, my friend, always welcome"—the two enthusiasts for science wrung hands—"and never more welcome than to-night. Then the great mystery is to be solved at last. The Theatre is crammed with people. What does it mean? You must tell me before you go in."

The Physicist smiled.

"I came to a conviction that I was on the true line five years ago," he said. "It is only within the last six months that I have demonstrated the thing to a certainty. I will tell you, my friend," he whispered, "before we go in."

Then he advanced and shook hands with the President.

"Whatever the importance of your Discovery, Professor," said the President, "we are fully sensible of the honor you have done us in bringing it before an English audience first of all, and especially before an audience of the Royal Institution."

"Ja, Ja, Herr President. But I give my Discovery to all the world at this same hour. As for myself, I announce it to my very good friends of the Royal Institution. Why not to my other very good friends of the Royal Society? Because it is a thing which belongs to the whole world, and not to scientific men only."

It was in the Library of the Royal Institution. The President and Council of the Institution were gathered together to receive their illustrious lecturer, and every face was touched with interrogation and anxiety. What was this Great Discovery?

For six months there had appeared, from time to time, mysterious telegrams in the papers, all connected with this industrious Professor's laboratory. Nothing definite, nothing certain: it was whispered that a new discovery, soon about to be announced, would entirely change the relations of man to man; of nation to nation. Those who professed to be in the secret suggested that it might alter all governments and abolish all laws. Why they said that I know not, because certainly nobody was admitted to the laboratory, and the Professor had no confidant. This big-headed man, with the enormous bald forehead and the big glasses on his fat nose—it was long and broad as well as fat—kept his own counsel. Yet, in some way, people were perfectly certain that something wonderful was coming. So, when Roger Bacon made his gunpowder, the monks might have whispered to each other, only from the smell which came through the key-hole, that now the Devil would at last be met upon his own ground. The telegrams were continued with exasperating pertinacity, until over the whole civilized world the eyes of all who loved science were turned upon that modest laboratory in the little University of Ganzweltweisst am Rhein. What was coming from it? One does not go so far as to say that all interest in contemporary business, politics, art, and letters ceased; but it is quite certain that every morning and every evening, when everybody opened his paper, his first thought was to look for news from Ganzweltweisst am Rhein.

But the days passed by, and no news came. This was especially hard on the leader-writers, who were one and all waiting, each man longing to have a cut in with the subject before anybody else got it. But it was good for the people who write letters to the papers, because they had so many opportunities of suggestion and surmise. And so the leader-writers got something to talk about after all. For some suggested that Prof. Schwarzbaum had found out a way to make food artificially, by chemically compounding nitrogens, phosphates, and so forth. And these philosophers built a magnificent Palace of Imagination, in which dwelt a glorified mankind no longer occupied in endless toil for the sake of providing meat and drink for themselves and their families, but all engaged in the pursuit of knowledge, and in Art of all kinds, such as Fiction, Poetry, Painting, Music, Acting, and so forth, getting out of Life such a wealth of emotion, pleasure, and culture as the world had never before imagined. Others there were who thought that the great Discovery might be a method of instantaneous transmission of matter from place to place; so that, as by the electric wire one can send a message, so by some kind of electric method one could send a human body from any one part of the world to any other in a moment. This suggestion offered a fine field for the imagination; and there was a novel written on this subject which had a great success, until the Discovery itself was announced. Others, again, thought that the new Discovery meant some great and wonderful development of the Destructive Art; so that the whole of an army might be blown into countless fragments by the touch of a button, the discharge of a spring, the fall of a hammer. This took the fancy hugely, and it was pleasant to read the imaginary developments of history as influenced by this Discovery. But it seemed certain that the learned Professor would keep it for the use of his own country. So that there was no longer any room to doubt that, if this was the nature of the Discovery, the whole of the habitable world must inevitably fall under the Teutonic yoke, and an Empire of Armed Peace would set in, the like of which had never before been witnessed upon the globe. On the whole, the prospect was received everywhere, except in France and Russia, with resignation. Even the United States remembered that they had already many millions of Germans among them; and that the new Empire, though it would give certainly all the places to these Germans, would also save them a great many Elections, and therefore a good deal of trouble, and would relieve the national conscience—long grievously oppressed in this particular—of truckling to the Irish Vote. Dynamiters and anarchists, however, were despondent, and Socialists regarded each other with an ever-deepening gloom. This particular Theory of the great Discovery met, in fact, with universal credence over the whole civilized globe.

From the great man himself there came no sign. Enterprising interviewers failed to get speech with him. Scientific men wrote to him, but got no real information in reply. And the minds of men grew more and more agitated. Some great change was considered certain—but what?

One morning—it was the morning of Thursday, June 20, 1890—there appeared an advertisement in the papers. By the telegrams it was discovered that a similar advertisement had been published in every great city all over the world. That of the London papers differed from others in one important respect—in this, namely: Professor Schwarzbaum would himself, without any delay, read before a London audience a Paper which should reveal his new Discovery. There was not, however, the least hint in the announcement of the nature of this Discovery.

"Yes," said the Physicist, speaking slowly, "I have given the particulars to my friends over the whole earth; and, as London is still the centre of the world, I resolved that I would myself communicate it to the English."

"But what is it?—what is it?" asked the President.

"The Discovery," the Professor continued, "is to be announced at the same moment all over the world, so that none of the newspapers shall have an unfair start. It is now close upon nine o'clock by London time. In Paris it is ten minutes past nine; in Berlin it is six minutes before ten; at St. Petersburg it is eleven o'clock; at New York it is four o'clock in the afternoon. Very good. When the clock in your theatre points to nine exactly, at that moment everywhere the same Paper will be read."

In fact, at that moment the clock began to strike. The President led the way to the Theatre, followed by the Council. The Director remained behind with the Lecturer of the evening.

"My friend," said Professor Schwarzbaum, "my subject is nothing less"—he laid his finger upon the Director's arm—"nothing less than 'The Prolongation of the Vital Energy.'"

"What! The Prolongation of the Vital Energy? Do you know what that means?" The Director turned pale. "Are we to understand—"

"Come," said the Professor, "we must not waste the time."

Then the Director, startled and pale, took his German brother by the arm and led him into the Theatre, murmuring, "Prolongation. . . Prolongation. . . Prolongation. . . of the Vital—the Vital—Energy!"

The Theatre was crowded. There was not a vacant seat: there was no more standing room on the stairs; the very doors of the gallery were thronged: the great staircase was thronged with those who could not get in, but waited to get the first news. Nay, outside the Institution, Albemarle Street was crowded with people waiting to hear what this great thing might be which all the world had waited six months to hear. Within the Theatre, what an audience! For the first time in English history, no respect at all had been paid to rank: the people gathered in the Theatre were all that the great City could boast that was distinguished in science, art, and letters. Those present were the men who moved the world. Among them, naturally, a sprinkling of the men who are born to the best things of the world, and are sometimes told that they help to move it. There were ladies among the company too—ladies well known in scientific and literary circles, with certain great ladies led by curiosity. On the left-hand side of the Theatre, for instance, close to the door, sat two very great ladies, indeed—one of them the Countess of Thordisá, and the other her only daughter, the Lady Mildred Carera. Leaning against the pillar beside them stood a young man of singularly handsome appearance, tall and commanding of stature.

"To you, Dr. Linister," said the Countess, "I suppose everything that the Professor has to tell us will be already well known?"

"That," said Dr. Linister, "would be too much to expect."

"For me," her Ladyship went on delicately, "I love to catch Science on the wing—on the wing—in her lighter moods, when she has something really popular to tell."

Dr. Linister bowed. Then his eyes met those of the beautiful girl sitting below him, and he leaned and whispered,

"I looked for you everywhere last night. You had led me to understand—"

"We went nowhere, after all. Mamma fancied she had a bad cold."

"Then this evening. May I be quite—quite sure?"

His voice dropped, and his fingers met hers beneath the fan. She drew them away quickly, with a blush.

"Yes," she whispered, "you may find me to-night at Lady Chatterton's or Lady Ingleby's."

From which you can understand that this young Dr. Linister was quite a man in society. He was young, he had already a great reputation for Biological research, he was the only son of a fashionable physician, and he would be very rich. Therefore, in the season, Harry Linister was *of* the season.

On most of the faces present there sat an expression of anxiety, and even fear. What was this new thing? Was the world really going to be turned upside down? And when the West End was so very comfortable and its position so very well assured! But there were a few present who rubbed their hands at the thought of a great upturn of everything. Up with the scum first; when that had been ladled overboard, a new arrangement would be possible, to the advantage of those who rubbed their hands.

When the clock struck nine, a dead silence fell upon the Theatre; not a breath was heard; not a cough; not the rustle of a dress. Their faces were pale with expectancy; their lips were parted; their very breathing seemed arrested.

Then the President and the Council walked in and took their places.

"Ladies and Gentlemen," said the President shortly, "the learned Professor will himself communicate to you the subject and title of his Paper, and we may be certain beforehand that this subject and matter will adorn the motto of the Society—*Illustrous commoda vitæ.*"

Then Dr. Schwarzbaum stood at the table before them all, and looked round the room. Lady Mildred glanced at the young man, Harry

Linister. He was staring at the German like the rest, speechless. She sighed. Women did not in those days like love-making to be forgotten or interrupted by anything, certainly not by science.

The learned German carried a small bundle of papers, which he laid on the table. He carefully and slowly adjusted his spectacles. Then he drew from his pocket a small leather case. Then he looked round the room and smiled. That is to say, his lips were covered with a full beard, so that the sweetness of the smile was mostly lost; but it was observed under and behind the beard. The mere ghost of a smile; yet a benevolent ghost.

The Lecturer began, somewhat in copy-book fashion, to remind his audience that everything in Nature is born, grows slowly to maturity, enjoys a brief period of full force and strength, then decays, and finally dies. The tree of life is first a green sapling, and last a white and leafless trunk. He expatiated at some length on the growth of the young life. He pointed out that methods had been discovered to hinder that growth, turn it into unnatural forms, even to stop and destroy it altogether. He showed how the body is gradually strengthened in all its parts; he showed, for his unscientific hearers, how the various parts of the structure assume strength. All this was familiar to most of his audience. Next he proceeded to dwell upon the period of full maturity of bodily and mental strength, which, in a man, should last from twenty-five to sixty, and even beyond that time. The decay of the bodily, and even of the mental organs, may have already set in, even when mind and body seem the most vigorous. At this period of the discussion most of the audience were beginning to flag in their attention. Was such a gathering as this assembled only to hear a discussion on the growth and decay of the faculties? But the Director, who knew what was coming, sat bolt upright, expectant. It was strange, the people said afterwards, that no one should have suspected what was coming. There was to be, everybody knew, a great announcement. That was certain. Destruction, Locomotion, Food, Transmission of Thought, Substitution of Speech for Writing—all these things, as has been seen, had been suggested. But no one even guessed the real nature of the Discovery. And now, with the exception of the people who always pretend to have known all along, to have been favored with the Great Man's Confidence, to have guessed the thing from the outset, no one had the least suspicion.

Therefore, when the Professor suddenly stopped short, after a prolix description of wasting power and wearied organs, and held up an admonitory finger, everybody jumped, because now the Secret was to be divulged. They had come to hear a great Secret.

"What is this Decay?" he asked. "What is it? Why does it begin? What laws regulate it? What check can we place upon it? How can we prevent it? How can we stay its progress? Can Science, which has done so much to make Life happy—which has found out so many things by which Man's brief span is crowded with delightful emotions—can Science do no more? Cannot Science add to these gifts that more precious gift of all—the lengthening of that brief span?"

Here everybody gasped.

"I ask," the speaker went on, "whether Science cannot put off that day which closes the eyes and turns the body into a senseless lump? Consider: we are no sooner arrived at the goal of our ambitions than we have to go away; we are no sooner at the plenitude of our wisdom and knowledge than we have to lay down all that we have learned and go away—nay, we cannot even transmit to others our accumulations of knowledge. They are lost. We are no sooner happy with those we love than we have to leave them. We collect, but cannot enjoy; we inherit—it is but for a day; we learn, but we have no time to use our learning; we love—it is but for an hour; we pass our youth in hope, our manhood in effort, and we die before we are old; we are strong, but our strength passes like a dream; we are beautiful, but our beauty perishes in a single day. Cannot, I ask again—cannot Science prolong the Vital Force, and stay the destroying hand of Decay?"

At this point a wonderful passion seized upon many of the people present; for some sprang to their feet and lifted hands and shouted, some wept aloud, some clasped each other by the hand; there were lovers among the crowd who fell openly into each other's arms; there were men of learning who hugged imaginary books and looked up with wild eyes; there were girls who smiled, thinking that their beauty might last longer than a day; there were women down whose cheeks rolled the tears of sorrow for their vanished beauty; there were old men who heard and trembled.

One of them spoke—out of all this crowd only one found words. It was an old statesman; an old man eloquent. He rose with shaking limbs.

"Sir," he cried, his voice still sonorous, "give me back my manhood!"

The Professor continued, regardless:

"Suppose," he said, "that Science had found out the way, not to restore what is lost, but to arrest further loss; not to give back what is gone—you might as well try to restore a leg that has been cut off—but to prevent further loss. Consider this for a moment, I pray you. Those who search into Nature's secrets might, if this were done for them, carry on their investigations far beyond any point which had yet been reached; those who cultivate Art might attain to a greater skill of hand and truth of sight than has ever yet been seen; those who study human nature might multiply their observations; those who love might have a longer time for their passion; men who are strong might remain strong; women who are beautiful might remain beautiful—"

"Sir," cried again the old man eloquent, "give me back my manhood!"

The Lecturer made no reply, but went on:

"The rich might have a time—a sensible length of time—in which to enjoy their wealth; the young might remain young; the old might grow no older; the feeble might not become more feeble—all for a prolonged time. As for those whose lives could never become anything but a burden to themselves and to the rest of the world—the crippled, the criminal, the poor, the imbecile, the incompetent, the stupid, and the frivolous—they would live out their allotted lives and die. It would be for the salt of the earth, for the flower of mankind, for the men strong of intellect and endowed above the common herd, that Science would reserve this precious gift."

"Give me back my manhood!" cried again the old man eloquent.

But he was not alone, for they all sprang to their feet together and cried aloud, shrieking, weeping, stretching forth hands, "Give—give—give!" But the Director, who knew that what was asked for would be given, sat silent and self-possessed.

The Speaker motioned them all to sit down again.

"I would not," he said, "limit this great gift to those alone whose intellect leads the world. I would extend it to all who help to make life beautiful and happy; to lovely women"—here the men heaved a sigh so deep, so simultaneous, that it fell upon the ear like the voice of thanksgiving from a Cathedral choir—"to those who love only the empty show and pleasures and vainglories of life"—here many smiled, especially of the younger sort—"even to some of those who desire nothing of life but love and song and dalliance and laughter." Again the younger sort smiled, and tried to look as if they had no connection at all with that band. "I would extend this gift, I repeat, to all who can themselves be happy in the sunshine and the light, and to all who can make the happiness of others. Then, again, consider. When you have enjoyed

WALTER BESANT

those things for a while; when your life has been prolonged, so that you have enjoyed all that you desire in full measure and running over; when not two or three years have passed, but perhaps two or three centuries, you would then, of your own accord, put aside the aid of Science and suffer your body to fall into the decay which awaits all living matter. Contented and resigned, you would sink into the tomb, not satiated with the joys of life, but satisfied to have had your share. There would be no terror in death, since it would take none but those who could say, 'I have had enough.' That day would surely come to every one. There is nothing—not research and discovery, not the beauty of Nature, not love and pleasure, not art, not flowers and sunshine and perpetual youth—of which we should not in time grow weary. Science cannot alter the Laws of Nature. Of all things there must be an end. But she can prolong; she can avert; she can—Yes, my friends. This is my Discovery; this is my Gift to Humanity; this is the fruit, the outcome of my life; for me this great thing has been reserved. Science can arrest decay. She can make you live—live on—live for centuries—nay, I know not—why not?—she can, if you foolishly desire it, make you live forever."

Now, when these words were spoken there fell a deep silence upon the crowd. No one spoke; no one looked up; they were awed; they could not realize what it meant that would be given them; they were suddenly relieved of a great terror, the constant dread that lies in man's heart, ever present, though we conceal it—the dread of Death; but they could not, in a moment, understand that it was given.

But the Director sprang to his feet, and grasped his brother physicist by the hand.

"Of all the sons of Science," he said, solemnly, "thou shalt be proclaimed the first and best."

The assembly heard these words, but made no sign. There was no applause—not a murmur, not a voice. They were stricken dumb with wonder and with awe. They were going to live—to live on—to live for centuries, nay, why not?—to live forever!

"You all know," the Professor continued, "how at a dinner a single glass of champagne revives the spirits, looses the tongue, and brings activity to the brain. The guests were weary; they were in decay; the Champagne arrests that decay. My discovery is of another kind of Champagne, which acts with a more lasting effect. It strengthens the nerves, hardens the muscles, quickens the blood, and brings activity to the digestion. With new strength of the body returns new strength to the mind; mind and body are one." He paused a moment. Then he gave the leather case into the hands of the Director. "This is my gift, I say. I give to my brother full particulars and the history of the invention. I seek no profit for myself. It is your own. This day a new epoch begins for humanity. We shall not die, but live. Accident, fire, lightning, may kill us. Against these things we cannot guard. But old age shall no more fall upon us; decay shall no more rob us of our life and strength; and death shall be voluntary. This is a great change. I know not if I have done aright. That is for you to determine. See that you use this gift aright."

Then, before the people had understood the last words, the speaker stepped out of the Theatre and was gone.

But the Director of the Royal Institution stood in his place, and in his hand was the leather case containing the GIFT OF LIFE.

THE COUNTESS OF THORDISÁ, WHO had been asleep throughout the lecture, woke up when it was finished.

"How deeply interesting!" she sighed. "This it is, to catch Science on the wing." Then she looked round. "Mildred, dear," she said, "has Dr. Linister gone to find the carriage? Dear me! what a commotion! And at the Royal Institution, of all places in the world!"

"I think, Mamma," said Lady Mildred, coldly, "that we had better get some one else to find the carriage. Dr. Linister is over there. He is better engaged."

He was; he was among his brother physicists; they were eagerly asking questions and crowding round the Director. And the Theatre seemed filled with mad people, who surged and crowded and pushed.

"Come, Mamma," said Lady Mildred, pale, but with a red spot on either cheek, "we will leave them to fight it out."

Science had beaten love. She did not meet Harry Linister again that night. And when they met again, long years afterwards, he passed her by with eyes that showed he had clean forgotten her existence, unaltered though she was in face and form.

I

The Supper-Bell

When the big bell in the Tower of the House of Life struck the hour of seven, the other bells began to chime as they had done every day at this hour for I know not how many years. Very likely in the Library, where we still keep a great collection of perfectly useless books, there is preserved some History which may speak of these Bells, and of the builders of the House. When these chimes began, the swifts and jackdaws which live in the Tower began to fly about with a great show of hurry, as if there was barely time for supper, though, as it was yet only the month of July, the sun would not be setting for an hour or more.

We have long since ceased to preach to the people, otherwise we might make them learn a great deal from the animal world. They live, for instance, from day to day; not only are their lives miserably short, but they are always hungry, always fighting, always quarrelling, always fierce in their loves and their jealousies. Watching the swifts, for instance, which we may do nearly all day long, we ought to congratulate ourselves on our own leisurely order, the adequate provision for food made by the Wisdom of the College, the assurance of preservation also established by that Wisdom, and our freedom from haste and anxiety, as from the emotions of love, hatred, jealousy, and rivalry. But the time has gone by for that kind of exhortation.

Thus, our people, who at this hour crowded the great Square, showed in their faces, their attitudes, and their movements, the calm that reigned in their souls. Some were lying on the grass; some were sitting on the benches; some were strolling. They were for the most part alone; if not alone—because habit often survives when the original cause of the habit is gone—then in pairs.

In the old unhappy days there would have been restless activity—a hurrying to and fro; there would have been laughter and talking—everybody would have been talking; there would have been young men eagerly courting the favors of young women, looking on them with longing eyes, ready to fight for them, each for the girl he loved; thinking each of the girl he loved as of a goddess or an angel—all perfection. The girls themselves ardently desired this foolish worship. Again, formerly, there would have been old men and old women looking with melancholy eyes on the scenes they were about to quit, and lamenting the days of their strength and their youth. And formerly there would have been among the crowd beggars and paupers; there would have been some masters and some servants; some noble and some bourgeois; there would have been every conceivable difference in age, rank, strength, intellect, and distinction.

Again, formerly there would have been the most insolent differences in costume. Some of the men used to wear broadcloth, sleek and smooth, with glossy hats and gloves, and flowers at their button-hole; while beside them crawled the wretched half-clad objects pretending to sell matches, but in reality begging for their bread. And some of the women used to flaunt in dainty and expensive stuffs, setting off their supposed charms (which were mostly made by the dress-maker's art) with the curves and colors of their drapery. And beside them would be crawling the wretched creatures to whom in the summer, when the days were hot and fine, the Park was their only home, and rusty black their only wear.

Now, no activity at all; no hurrying, no laughing, not even any talking. That might have struck a visitor as one of the most remarkable results of our system. No foolish talking. As for their dress, it was all alike. The men wore blue flannel jackets and trousers, with a flannel shirt and a flat blue cap; for the working hours they had a rougher dress. The women wore a costume in gray, made of a stuff called beige. It is a useful stuff, because it wears well; it is soft and yet warm, and cannot be objected to by any of them on the score of ugliness. What mutinies, what secret conspiracies, what mad revolts had to be faced before the women could be made to understand that Socialism—the only form of society which can now be accepted—must be logical and complete! What is one woman more than another that she should separate herself from her sisters by her dress? Therefore, since their subjugation they all wear a gray beige frock, with a jacket of the same, and a flat gray cap, like the men's, under which they are made to gather up their hair.

This scene, indeed—the gathering of the People before the supper-bell—is one of which I never tire. I look at all the eager, hurrying swifts in the air, I remember the Past; and I think of the Present when I gaze upon the great multitude, in which no one regardeth his neighbor, none speaks to none. There are no individual aims, but all is pure, unadulterated Socialism, with—not far distant—the Ultimate Triumph of Science!

I desire to relate the exact circumstances connected with certain recent events. It is generally known that they caused one deplorable Death—one of our own Society, although not a Physician of the HOUSE. I shall have to explain, before I begin the narrative, certain points in our internal management which may differ from the customs adopted elsewhere. We of the Later Era visit each other so seldom that differences may easily grow up. Indeed, considering the terrible dangers of travel—how, if one walks, there are the perils of unfiltered water, damp beds, sprained ankles, byrsitis of the knee, chills from frosts and showers; or if one gets into a wheeled vehicle, the wheels may fall off, or the carriage may be overturned in a ditch. . . But why pursue the subject? I repeat, therefore, that I must speak of the community and its order, but that as briefly as may be.

The Rebels have been driven forth from the Pale of Humanity to wander where they please. In a few years they will be released—if that has not already happened—by Death from the diseases and sufferings which will fall upon them. Then we shall remember them no more. The centuries will roll by, and they shall be forgotten; the very mounds of earth which once marked the place of their burial will be level with the ground around them. But the HOUSE and the Glory of the HOUSE will continue.

Thus perish all the enemies of Science!

The City of Canterbury, as it was rebuilt when Socialism was finally established, has in its centre a great Square, Park, or Garden, the central breathing-place and relaxation ground of the City. Each side is exactly half a mile in length. The Garden, thus occupying an area of a fourth of a square mile, is planted with every kind of ornamental tree, and laid out in flower-beds, winding walks, serpentine rivers, lakes, cascades, bridges, grottos, summer-houses, lawns, and everything that can help to make the place attractive. During the summer it is thronged every evening with the people. On its west side has been erected an enormous Palace of glass, low in height, but stretching far away to the west, covering an immense area. Here the heat is artificially maintained at temperatures varying with the season and the plants that are in cultivation. In winter, frost, bad weather, and in rain, it forms a place of recreation and rest. Here grow all kinds of fruit-trees, with all kinds of vegetables, flowers, and plants. All the year round it furnishes, in quantities sufficient for all our wants, an endless supply of fruit; so that we have a supply of some during the whole year, as grapes, bananas, and oranges; others for at least half the year, as peaches, strawberries, and so forth; while of the commoner vegetables, as peas, beans, and the like, there is now no season, but they are grown continuously. In the old times we were dependent upon the changes and chances of a capricious and variable climate. Now, not only has the erection of these vast houses made us independent of summer and winter, but the placing of much grass and corn land under glass has also assured our crops and secured us from the danger of famine. This is by no means one of the least advantages of modern civilization.

On the South side of the Square stands our Public Hall. The building has not, like the House of Life, any architectural beauty—why should we aim at beauty, when efficiency is our sole object? The House of Life was designed and erected when men thought perpetually of beauty, working from their admiration of beauty in woman and in nature to beauty in things which they made with their own hands, setting beauty above usefulness; even thinking it necessary, when usefulness had been attained, to add adornment, as when they added a Tower to the House of Life, yet did nothing with their Tower and did not want it.

The Public Hall is built of red brick; it resembles a row of houses each with a gable to the street. There is for each a broad plain door, with a simple porch, below; and above, a broad plain window twenty feet wide divided into four compartments or divisions, the whole set in a framework of wood. The appearance of the Hall is, therefore, remarkably plain. There are thirty-one of these gables, each forty feet wide; so that the whole length of the Hall is twelve hundred and forty feet, or nearly a quarter of a mile.

Within, the roof of each of these gables covers a Hall separated from its neighbors by plain columns. They are all alike, except that the middle Hall, set apart for the College, has a gallery originally intended for an orchestra, now never used. In the central Hall one table alone is placed; in all the others there are four, every Hall accommodating eight hundred people and every table two hundred. The length of each Hall is the same—namely, two hundred and fifty feet. The Hall is lit by one large window at each end. There are no carvings, sculptures, or other ornaments in the building. At the back is an extensive range of buildings, all of brick, built in small compartments, and fire-proof; they contain the kitchens, granaries, *abattoirs*, larders, cellars, dairies, still-rooms, pantries, curing-houses, ovens, breweries, and all the other offices and chambers required for the daily provisioning of a city with twenty-four thousand inhabitants.

On the East side of the Square there are two great groups of buildings. That nearest to the Public Hall contains, in a series of buildings which communicate with one another, the Library, the Museum, the Armory, the Model-room, and the Picture Gallery. The last is a building as old as the House. They were, when these events began, open to the whole Community, though they were never visited by any even out of idle curiosity. The inquisitive spirit is dead. For myself, I am not anxious to see the people acquire, or revive, the habit of reading and inquiring. It might be argued that the study of history might make them contrast the present with the past, and shudder at the lot of their forefathers. But I am going to show that this study may produce quite the opposite effect. Or, there is the study of science. How should this help the People? They have the College always studying and investigating for their benefit the secrets of medical science, which alone concerns their happiness. They might learn how to make machines; but machinery requires steam, explosives, electricity, and other uncontrolled and dangerous forces. Many thousands of lives were formerly lost in the making and management of these machines, and we do very well without them. They might, it is true, read the books which tell of the people in former times. But why read works which are filled with the Presence of Death, the Shortness of Life, and the intensity of passions which we have almost forgotten? You shall see what comes of these studies which seem so innocent.

I say, therefore, that I never had any wish to see the people flocking into the Library. For the same reason—that a study and contemplation of things past might unsettle or disturb the tranquillity of their minds—I have never wished to see them in the Museum, the Armory, or any other part of our Collections. And since the events of which I have to tell, we have enclosed these buildings and added them to the College, so that the people can no longer enter them even if they wished.

The Curator of the Museum was an aged man, one of the few old men left—in the old days he had held a title of some kind. He was placed there because he was old and much broken, and could do no work. Therefore he was told to keep the glass-cases free from dust and to sweep the floors every morning. At the time of the Great Discovery he had been an Earl or Viscount—I know not what—and by some accident he escaped the Great Slaughter, when it was resolved to kill all the old men and women in order to reduce the population to the number which the land would support. I believe that he hid himself, and was secretly fed by some man who had formerly been his groom, and still preserved some remains of what he called attachment and duty, until such time as the executions were over. Then he ventured forth again, and so great was the horror of the recent massacre, with the recollection of the prayers and shrieks of the victims, that he was allowed to continue alive. The old man was troubled with an asthma which hardly permitted him an hour of repose and was incurable. This would have made his life intolerable, except that to live—only to live, in any pain and misery—is always better than to die.

For the last few years the old man had a companion in the Museum. This was a girl—the only girl in our Community—who called him—I know not why (perhaps because the relationship really existed)—Grandfather, and lived with him. She it was who dusted the cases and swept the floors. She found some means of relieving the old man's asthma, and all day long—would that I had discovered the fact, or suspected whither it would lead the wretched girl!—she read the books of the Library and studied the contents of the cases and talked to the old man, making him tell her everything that belonged to the past. All she cared for was the Past; all that she studied was to understand more and more—how men lived then, and what they thought, and what they talked.

She was about eighteen years of age; but, indeed, we thought her still a child. I know not how many years had elapsed since any in the City were children, because it is a vain thing to keep account of the years; if anything happens to distinguish them, it must be something disastrous, because we have now arrived almost at the last stage possible to man. It only remains for us to discover, not only how to prevent disease, but how to annihilate it. Since, then, there is only one step left to take in advance, every other event which can happen must be in the nature of a calamity, and therefore may be forgotten.

I have said that Christine called the old man her grandfather. We have long, long since agreed to forget old ties of blood. How can father and son, mother and daughter, brother and sister continue for hundreds of years, and when all remain fixed at the same age, to keep up the old relationship? The maternal love dies out with us—it is now but seldom called into existence—when the child can run about. Why not? The animals, from whom we learn so much, desert their offspring when they can feed themselves; our mothers cease to care for their children when they are old enough to be the charge of the Community. Therefore Christine's mother cheerfully suffered the child to leave her as soon as she was old enough to sit in the Public Hall. Her grandfather—if indeed he was her grandfather—obtained permission to have the child with him. So she remained in the quiet Museum. We never imagined or suspected, however, that the old man, who was eighty at the time of the Great Discovery, remembered everything that took place when he was young, and talked with the girl all day long about the Past.

I do not know who was Christine's father. It matters not now; and, indeed, he never claimed his daughter. One smiles to think of the importance formerly attached to fathers. We no longer work for their support. We are no longer dependent upon their assistance; the father does nothing for the son, nor the son for the father. Five hundred years ago, say—or a thousand years ago—the father carried a baby in his arms. What then? My own father—I believe he is my own father, but on this point I may be mistaken—I saw yesterday taking his turn in the hay-field. He seemed distressed with the heat and fatigue of it. Why not? It makes no difference to me. He is, though not so young, still as strong and as able-bodied as myself. Christine was called into existence by the sanction of the College when one of the Community was struck dead by lightning. It was my brother, I believe. The terrible event filled us all with consternation. However, the population having thus been diminished by one, it was resolved that the loss should be repaired. There was precedent. A great many years previously, owing to a man being killed by the fall of a hay-rick—all hay-ricks are now made low—another birth had been allowed. That was a boy.

Let us now return to our Square. On the same side are the buildings of the College. Here are the Anatomical collections, the storehouse of Materia Medica, and the residences of the Arch Physician, the Suffragan, the Fellows of the College or Associate Physicians, and the Assistants or Experimenters. The buildings are plain and fire-proof. The College has its own private gardens, which are large and filled with trees. Here the Physicians walk and meditate, undisturbed by the outer world. Here is also their Library.

On the North side of the Square stands the great and venerable House of Life, the Glory of the City, the Pride of the whole Country.

It is very ancient. Formerly there were many such splendid monuments standing in the country; now this alone remains. It was built in the dim, distant ages, when men believed things now forgotten. It was designed for the celebration of certain ceremonies or functions; their nature and meaning may, I dare say, be ascertained by any who cares to waste time in an inquiry so useless. The edifice itself could not possibly be built in these times; first because we have no artificers capable of rearing such a pile, and next because we have not among us any one capable of conceiving it, or drawing the design of it; nay, we have none who could execute the carved stone-work.

I do not say this with humility, but with satisfaction; for, if we contemplate the building, we must acknowledge that, though it is, as I have said, the Glory of the City, and though it is vast in proportions, imposing by its grandeur, and splendid in its work, yet most of it is perfectly useless. What need of the tall columns to support a roof which might very well have been one-fourth the present height? Why build the Tower at all? What is the good of the carved work? We of the New Era build in brick, which is fire-proof; we put up structures which are no larger than are wanted; we waste no labor, because we grudge the time which must be spent in necessary work, over things unnecessary. Besides, we are no longer tortured by the feverish anxiety to do something—anything—by which we may be remembered when the short span of life is past. Death to us is a thing which may happen by accident, but not from old age or by disease. Why should men toil and trouble in order to be remembered? All things are equal: why should one man try to do something better than another—or what another cannot do—or what is useless when it is done? Sculptures, pictures, Art of any kind, will not add a single ear of corn to the general stock, or a single glass of wine, or a yard of flannel. Therefore, we need not regret the decay of Art.

As everybody knows, however, the House is the chief Laboratory of the whole country. It is here that the Great Secret is preserved; it is known to the Arch Physician and to his Suffragan alone. No other man in the country knows by what process is compounded that potent liquid which arrests decay and prolongs life, apparently without any bound or limit. I say without any bound or limit. There certainly are croakers, who maintain that at some future time—it may be this very year, it may be a thousand years hence—the compound will lose its power, and so we—all of us, even the College—must then inevitably begin to decay, and after a few short years perish and sink into the silent grave. The very thought causes a horror too dreadful for words; the limbs tremble, the teeth chatter. But others declare that there is no fear whatever of this result, and that the only dread is lest the whole College should suddenly be struck by lightning, and so the Secret be lost. For though none other than the Arch Physician and his Suffragan know the Secret, the whole Society—the Fellows or Assistant Physicians—know in what strong place the Secret is kept in writing, just as it was communicated by the Discoverer. The Fellows of the College all assist in the production of this precious liquid, which is made only in the HOUSE OF LIFE. But none of them know whether they are working for the great Arcanum itself, or on some of the many experiments conducted for the Arch Physician. Even if one guessed, he would not dare to communicate his suspicions even to a Brother-Fellow, being forbidden, under the most awful of all penalties, that of Death itself, to divulge the experiments and processes that he is ordered to carry out.

It is needless to say that if we are proud of the HOUSE, we are equally proud of the City. There was formerly an old Canterbury, of which pictures exist in the Library. The streets of that town were narrow and winding; the houses were irregular in height, size, and style. There were close courts, not six feet broad, in which no air could circulate, and where fevers and other disorders were bred. Some houses, again, stood in stately gardens, while others had none at all; and the owners of the gardens kept them closed. But we can easily understand what might have happened when private property was recognized, and laws protected the so-called rights of owners. Now that there is no property, there are no laws. There are also no crimes, because there is no incentive to jealousy, rapine, or double-dealing. Where there is no crime, there is that condition of Innocence which our ancestors so eagerly desired, and sought by means which were perfectly certain to fail.

How different is the Canterbury of the present! First, like all modern towns, it is limited in size; there are in it twenty-four thousand inhabitants, neither more nor less. Round its great central Square or Garden are the public buildings. The streets, which branch off at right angles, are all of the same width, the same length, and the same appearance. They are planted with trees. The houses are built of red brick, each house containing four rooms on the ground-floor—namely, two on either side the door—and four on the first floor, with a bath-room. The rooms are vaulted with brick, so that there is no fear of fire. Every room has its own occupant; and as all the rooms are of the same size, and are all furnished in the same way, with the same regard to comfort and warmth, there is really no ground for complaint or jealousies. The occupants also, who have the same meals in the same Hall every day, cannot complain of inequalities, any more than they can accuse each other of gluttonous living. In the matter of clothes, again, it was at first expected that the grave difficulties with the women as to uniformity of fashion and of material would continue to trouble us; but with the decay of those emotions which formerly caused so much trouble—since the men have ceased to court the women, and the women have ceased to desire men's admiration—there has been no opposition. All of them now are clad alike; gray is found the most convenient color, soft beige the most convenient material.

The same beautiful equality rules the hours and methods of work. Five hours a day are found ample, and everybody takes his time at every kind of work, the men's work being kept separate from that given to the women. I confess that the work is not performed with as much zeal as one could wish; but think of the old times, when one had to work eight, ten, and even eighteen hours a day in order to earn a poor and miserable subsistence! What zeal could they have put into their work? How different is this glorious equality in all things from the ancient anomalies and injustices of class and rank, wealth and poverty! Why, formerly, the chief pursuit of man was the pursuit of money. And now there is no money at all, and our wealth lies in our barns and garners.

I must be forgiven if I dwell upon these contrasts. The history which has to be told—how an attempt was actually made to destroy this Eden, and to substitute in its place the old condition of things—fills me with such indignation that I am constrained to speak.

Consider, for one other thing, the former condition of the world. It was filled with diseases. People were not in any way protected. They were allowed to live as they pleased. Consequently, they all committed excesses and all contracted disease. Some drank too much, some ate too much, some took no exercise, some took too little, some lay in bed too long, some went to bed too late, some suffered themselves to fall into violent rages, into remorse, into despair; some loved inordinately; thousands worked too hard. All ran after Jack-o'-Lanterns continually; for, before one there was dangled the hope of promotion, before another that of glory, before another that of distinction, fame, or praise; before another that of wealth, before another the chance of retiring to rest and meditate during the brief remainder of his life—miserably short even in its whole length. Then diseases fell upon them, and they died.

WALTER BESANT

We have now prevented all new diseases, though we cannot wholly cure those which have so long existed. Rheumatism, gout, fevers, arise no more, though of gout and other maladies there are hereditary cases. And since there are no longer any old men among us, there are none of the maladies to which old age is liable. No more pain, no more suffering, no more anxiety, no more Death (except by accident) in the world. Yet some of them would return to the old miseries; and for what?—for what? You shall hear.

WHEN THE CHIMES BEGAN, THE people turned their faces with one consent towards the Public Hall, and a smile of satisfaction spread over all their faces. They were going to Supper—the principal event of the day. At the same moment a Procession issued from the iron gates of the College. First marched our Warder, or Porter, John Lax, bearing a halberd; next came an Assistant, carrying a cushion, on which were the Keys of Gold, symbolical of the Gate of Life; then came another, bearing our banner, with the Labarum or symbol of Life: the Assistants followed, in ancient garb of cap and gown; then came the twelve Fellows or Physicians of the College, in scarlet gowns and flat fur-lined caps; after them, I myself—Samuel Grout, M.D., Suffragan—followed. Last, there marched the first Person in the Realm—none other than the Arch Physician Himself, Dr. Henry Linister, in lawn sleeves, a black silk gown, and a scarlet hood. Four Beadles closed the Procession; for, with us, the only deviation from equality absolute is made in the case of the College. We are a Caste apart; we keep mankind alive and free from pain. This is our work; this occupies all our thoughts. We are, therefore, held in honor, and excused the ordinary work which the others must daily perform. And behold the difference between ancient and modern times! For, formerly, those who were held in honor and had high office in this always sacred HOUSE were aged and white-haired men who arrived at this distinction but a year or two before they had to die. But we of the Holy College are as stalwart, as strong, and as young as any man in the Hall. And so have we been for hundreds of years, and so we mean to continue.

In the Public Hall, we take our meals apart in our own Hall; yet the food is the same for all. Life is the common possession; it is maintained for all by the same process—here must be no difference. Let all, therefore, eat and drink alike.

When I consider, I repeat, the universal happiness, I am carried away, first, with a burning indignation that any should be so mad as to mar this happiness. They have failed; but they cost us, as you shall hear, much trouble, and caused the lamentable death of a most zealous and able officer.

Among the last to enter the gates were the girl Christine and her grandfather, who walked slowly, coughing all the way.

"Come, grandad," she said, as we passed her, "take my arm. You will be better after your dinner. Lean on me."

There was in her face so remarkable a light that I wonder now that no suspicion or distrust possessed us. I call it light, for I can compare it to nothing else. The easy, comfortable life our people led, and the absence of all exciting work, the decay of reading, and the abandonment of art, had left their faces placid to look upon, but dull. They were certainly dull. They moved heavily; if they lifted their eyes, they wanted the light that flashed from Christine's. It was a childish face still—full of softness. No one would ever believe that a creature so slight in form, so gentle to look upon, whose eyes were so soft, whose cheeks were like the untouched bloom of a ripe peach, whose half-parted lips were so rosy, was already harboring thoughts so abominable and already conceiving an enterprise so wicked.

We do not suspect, in this our new World. As we have no property to defend, no one is a thief; as everybody has as much of everything as he wants, no one tries to get more; we fear not Death, and therefore need no religion; we have no private ambitions to gratify, and no private ends to attain; therefore we have long since ceased to be suspicious. Least of all should we have been suspicious of Christine. Why, but a year or two ago she was a little newly born babe, whom the Holy College crowded to see as a new thing. And yet, was it possible that one so young should be so corrupt?

"Suffragan," said the Arch Physician to me at supper, "I begin to think that your Triumph of Science must be really complete."

"Why, Physician?"

"Because, day after day, that child leads the old man by the hand, places him in his seat, and ministers, after the old, forgotten fashion, to his slightest wants, and no one pays her the slightest heed."

"Why should they?"

"A child—a beautiful child! A feeble old man! One who ministers to another. Suffragan, the Past is indeed far, far away; but I knew not until now that it was so utterly lost. Childhood and Age and the offices of Love! And these things are wholly unheeded. Grout, you are indeed a great man!"

He spoke in the mocking tone which was usual with him, so that we never knew exactly whether he was in earnest or not; but I think that on this occasion he was in earnest. No one but a very great man—none smaller than Samuel Grout—myself—could have accomplished this miracle upon the minds of the People. They did not minister one to the other. Why should they? Everybody could eat his own ration without any help. Offices of Love? These to pass unheeded? What did the Arch Physician mean?

II

Grout, Suffragan

It always pleases me, from my place at the College table, which is raised two feet above the rest, to contemplate the multitude whom it is our duty and our pleasure to keep in contentment and in health. It is a daily joy to watch them flocking, as you have seen them flock, to their meals. The heart glows to think of what we have done. I see the faces of all light up with satisfaction at the prospect of the food; it is the only thing that moves them. Yes, we have reduced life to its simplest form. Here is true happiness. Nothing to hope, nothing to fear—except accident; a little work for the common preservation; a body of wise men always devising measures for the common good; food plentiful and varied; gardens for repose and recreation, both summer and winter; warmth, shelter, and the entire absence of all emotions. Why, the very faces of the People are growing all alike—one face for the men, and another for the women; perhaps in the far-off future the face of the man will approach nearer and nearer to that of the woman, and so all will be at last exactly alike, and the individual will exist, indeed, no more. Then there will be, from first to last, among the whole multitude neither distinction nor difference.

It is a face which fills one with contentment, though it will be many centuries before it approaches completeness. It is a smooth face, there are no lines in it; it is a grave face, the lips seldom smile, and never laugh; the eyes are heavy, and move slowly; there has already been achieved, though the change has been very gradual, the complete banishment of that expression which has been preserved in every one of the ancient portraits, which may be usefully studied for purposes of contrast. Whatever the emotion attempted to be portrayed, and even when the face was supposed to be at rest, there was always behind, visible to the eye, an expression of anxiety or eagerness. Some kind of pain always lies upon those old faces, even upon the youngest. How could it be otherwise? On the morrow they would be dead. They had to crowd into a few days whatever they could grasp of life.

As I sit there and watch our People at dinner, I see with satisfaction that the old pain has gone out of their faces. They have lived so long that they have forgotten Death. They live so easily that they are contented with life: we have reduced existence to the simplest. They eat and drink—it is their only pleasure; they work—it is a necessity for health and existence—but their work takes them no longer than till noontide; they lie in the sun, they sit in the shade, they sleep. If they had once any knowledge, it is now forgotten; their old ambitions, their old desires, all are forgotten. They sleep and eat, they work and rest. To rest and to eat are pleasures which they never desire to end. To live forever, to eat and drink forever—this is now their only hope. And this has been accomplished for them by the Holy College. Science has justified herself—this is the outcome of man's long search for generations into the secrets of Nature. We, who have carried on this search, have at length succeeded in stripping humanity of all those things which formerly made existence intolerable to him. He lives, he eats, he sleeps. Perhaps—I know not, but of this we sometimes talk in the College—I say, perhaps—we may succeed in making some kind of artificial food, as we compound the great Arcanum, with simple ingredients and without labor. We may also extend the duration of sleep; we may thus still further simplify existence. Man in the end—as I propose to make and mould the People—will sleep until Nature calls upon him to awake and eat. He will then eat, drink, and sleep again, while the years roll by. He will lie heedless of all; he will be heedless of the seasons, heedless of the centuries. Time will have no meaning for him—a breathing, living, inarticulate mass will be all that is left of the active, eager, chattering Man of the Past.

This may be done in the future, when yonder laboratory, which we call the House of Life, shall yield the secrets of Nature deeper and deeper still. At present we have arrived at this point—the chief pleasure of life is to eat and to drink. We have taught the People so much, of all the tastes which formerly gratified man this alone remains. We provide them daily with a sufficiency and variety of food; there are so many kinds of food, and the combinations are so endless, that practically the choice of our cooks is unlimited. Good food, varied food, well-cooked food, with drink also varied and pure, and the best that can be made, make our public meals a daily joy. We have learned to make all kinds of wine from the grapes in our hot-houses. It is so abundant that every day, all the year round, the People may call for a ration of what they please. We make also beer of every kind, cider, perry, and mead. The gratification of the sense of taste helps to remove the incentive to restlessness or discontent. The minds of most are occupied by no other thought than that of the last feast and the next; if they were to revolt, where would they find their next meal? At the outset we had, I confess, grave difficulties. There was not in existence any Holy College. We drifted without object or purpose. For a long time the old ambitions remained; the old passions were continued; the old ideas of private property prevailed; the old inequalities were kept up. Presently there arose from those who had no property the demand for a more equal share. The cry was fiercely resisted; then there followed civil war for a space, till both sides were horrified by the bloodshed that followed. Time also was on the side of them who rebelled. I was one, because at the time when the whole nation was admitted to a participation in the great Arcanum, I was myself a young man of nineteen, employed as a washer of bottles in Dr. Linister's laboratory, and therefore, according to the ideas of the time, a very humble person. Time helped us in an unexpected way. Property was in the hands of single individuals. Formerly they died and were succeeded by their sons; now the sons grew tired of waiting. How much longer were their fathers, who grew no older, to keep all the wealth to themselves? Therefore, the civil war having come to an end, with no result except a barren peace, the revolutionary party was presently joined by all but the holders of property, and the State took over to itself the whole wealth—that is to say, the whole land; there is no other wealth. Since that time there has been no private property; for since it was clearly unjust to take away from the father in order to give it to the son, with no limitation as to the time of enjoyment, everything followed the land—great houses, which were allowed to fall into ruin; pictures and works of art, libraries, jewels, which are in Museums; and money, which, however, ceased to be of value as soon as there was nothing which could be bought.

As for me, I was so fortunate as to perceive—Dr. Linister daily impressed it upon me—that of all occupations, that of Physicist would very quickly become the most important. I therefore remained in my employment, worked, read, experimented, and learned all that my master had to teach me. The other professions, indeed, fell into decay more speedily than some of us expected. There could be no more lawyers when there was no more property. Even libel, which was formerly the cause of many actions, became harmless when a man could not be injured; and, besides, it is impossible to libel any man when there are no longer any rules of conduct except the one duty of work, which is done in the eyes of all and cannot be shirked. And how could

Religion survive the removal of Death to some possible remote future? They tried, it is true, to keep up the pretence of it, and many, especially women, clung to the old forms of faith for I know not how long. With the great mass, religion ceased to have any influence as soon as life was assured. As for Art, Learning, Science—other than that of Physics, Biology, and Medicine—all gradually decayed and died away. And the old foolish pursuit of Literature, which once occupied so many, and was even held in a kind of honor—the writing of histories, poems, dramas, novels, essays on human life—this also decayed and died, because men ceased to be anxious about their past or their future, and were at last contented to dwell in the present.

Another and a most important change which may be noted was the gradual decline and disappearance of the passion called Love. This was once a curious and inexplicable yearning—so much is certain—of two young people towards each other, so that they were never content unless they were together, and longed to live apart from the rest of the world, each trying to make the other happier. At least, this is as I read history. For my own part, as I was constantly occupied with Science, I never felt this passion; or if I did, then I have quite forgotten it. Now, at the outset people who were in love rejoiced beyond measure that their happiness would last so long. They began, so long as the words had any meaning, to call each other Angels, Goddesses, Divinely Fair, possessed of every perfect gift, with other extravagancies, at the mere recollection of which we should now blush. Presently they grew tired of each other; they no longer lived apart from the rest of the world. They separated; or, if they continued to walk together, it was from force of habit. Some still continue thus to sit side by side. No new connections were formed. People ceased desiring to make others happy, because the State began to provide for everybody's happiness. The whole essence of the old society was a fight. Everybody fought for existence. Everybody trampled on the weaker. If a man loved a woman, he fought for her as well as for himself. Love? Why, when the true principle of life is recognized—the right of every individual to his or her share—and that an equal share in everything—and when the continuance of life is assured—what room is there for love? The very fact of the public life—the constant companionship, the open mingling of women with men, and this for year after year—the same women with the same men—has destroyed the mystery which formerly hung about womanhood, and was in itself the principal cause of love.

It is gone, therefore, and with it the most disturbing element of life. Without love, without ambition, without suffering, without religion, without quarrelling, without private rights, without rank or class, life is calm, gentle, undisturbed. Therefore, they all sit down to dinner in peace and contentment, every man's mind intent upon nothing but the bill of fare.

This evening, directed by the observation of the Arch Physician, I turned my eyes upon the girl Christine, who sat beside her grandfather. I observed, first—but the fact inspired me with no suspicion—that she was no longer a child, but a woman grown; and I began to wonder when she would come with the rest for the Arcanum. Most women, when births were common among us, used to come at about five-and-twenty; that is to say, in the first year or two of full womanhood, before their worst enemies—where there were two women, in the old days, there were two enemies—could say that they had begun to fall off. If you look round our table, you will see very few women older than twenty-four, and very few men older than thirty. There were many women at this table who might, perhaps, have been called beautiful in the old times; though now the men had ceased to think of beauty, and the women had ceased to desire admiration. Yet, if regular features, large eyes, small mouths, a great quantity of hair, and a rounded figure are beautiful, then there were many at the table who might have been called beautiful. But the girl Christine—I observed the fact with scientific interest—was so different from the other women that she seemed another kind of creature.

Her eyes were soft; there is no scientific term to express this softness of youth—one observes it especially in the young of the *cervus* kind. There was also a curious softness on her cheek, as if something would be rubbed away if one touched it. And her voice differed from that of her elder sisters; it was curiously gentle, and full of that quality which may be remarked in the wood-dove when she pairs in spring. They used to call it tenderness; but, since the thing itself disappeared, the word has naturally fallen out of use.

Now, I might have observed with suspicion, whereas I only remarked it as something strange, that the company among which Christine and the old man sat were curiously stirred and uneasy. They were disturbed out of their habitual tranquillity because the girl was discoursing to them. She was telling them what she had learned about the Past.

"Oh," I heard her say, "it was a beautiful time! Why did they ever

WALTER BESANT

suffer it to perish? Do you mean that you actually remember nothing of it?"

They looked at each other sheepishly.

"There were soldiers—men were soldiers; they went out to fight, with bands of music and the shouts of the people. There were whole armies of soldiers—thousands of them. They dressed in beautiful glittering clothes. Do you forget that?"

One of the men murmured, hazily, that there were soldiers.

"And there were sailors, who went upon the sea in great ships. Jack Carera"—she turned to one of them—"you are a sailor, too. You ought to remember."

"I remember the sailors very well indeed," said this young man, readily.

I always had my doubts about the wisdom of admitting our sailors among the People. We have a few ships for the carriage of those things which as yet we have not succeeded in growing for ourselves; these are manned by a few hundred sailors who long ago volunteered, and have gone on ever since. They are a brave race, ready to face the most terrible dangers of tempest and shipwreck; but they are also a dangerous, restless, talkative, questioning tribe. They have, in fact, preserved almost as much independence as the College itself. They are now confined to their own port of Sheerness.

Then the girl began to tell some pestilent story of love and shipwreck and rescue; and at hearing it some of them looked puzzled and some pained; but the sailor listened with all his ears.

"Where did you get that from, Christine?"

"Where I get everything—from the old Library. Come and read it in the book, Jack."

"I am not much hand at reading. But some day, perhaps after next voyage, Christine."

The girl poured out a glass of claret for the old man. Then she went on telling them stories; but most of her neighbors seemed neither to hear nor to comprehend. Only the sailor-man listened and nodded. Then she laughed out loud.

At this sound, so strange, so unexpected, everybody within hearing jumped. Her table was in the Hall next to our own, so that we heard the laugh quite plainly.

The Arch Physician looked round approvingly.

"How many years since we heard a good, honest *young* laugh, Suffragan? Give us more children, and soften our hearts for us. But, no;

the heart you want is the hard, crusted, selfish heart. See! No one asks why she laughed. They are all eating again now, just as if nothing had happened. Happy, enviable People!"

Presently he turned to me and remarked, in his lofty manner, as if he was above all the world,

"You cannot explain, Suffragan, why, at an unexpected touch, a sound, a voice, a trifle, the memory may be suddenly awakened to things long, long past and forgotten. Do you know what that laugh caused me to remember? I cannot explain why, nor can you. It recalled the evening of the Great Discovery—not the Discovery itself, but quite another thing. I went there more to meet a girl than to hear what the German had to say. As to that I expected very little. To meet that girl seemed of far more importance. I meant to make love to her—love, Suffragan—a thing which you can never understand—real, genuine love! I meant to marry her. Well, I did meet her; and I arranged for a convenient place where we could meet again after the Lecture. Then came the Discovery; and I was carried away, body and soul, and forgot the girl and love and everything in the stupefaction of this most wonderful Discovery, of which we have made, between us, such admirable use."

You never knew whether the Arch Physician was in earnest or not. Truly, we had made a most beautiful use of the Discovery; but it was not in the way that Dr. Linister would have chosen.

"All this remembered just because a girl laughed! Suffragan, Science cannot explain all."

I shall never pretend to deny that Dr. Linister's powers as a physicist were of the first order, nor that his Discoveries warranted his election to the Headship of the College. Yet, something was due, perhaps, to his tall and commanding figure, and to the look of authority which reigned naturally on his face, and to the way in which he always stepped into the first rank. He was always the Chief, long before the College of Physicians assumed the whole authority, in everything that he joined. He opposed the extinction of property, and would have had everybody win what he could, and keep it as long as he would; he opposed the Massacre of the Old; he was opposed, in short, to the majority of the College. Yet he was our Chief. His voice was clear, and what he said always produced its effect, though it did not upset my solid majority, or thwart the Grand Advance of the Triumph of Science. As for me, my position has been won by sheer work and merit. My figure is not commanding; I am short-sighted and dark-visaged; my voice is rough;

and as for manners, I have nothing to do with them. But in Science there is but one second to Linister—and that is Grout.

When the supper came to an end, we rose and marched back to the College in the same state and order with which we had arrived. As for the people, some of them went out into the Garden; some remained in the Hall. It was then nine o'clock, and twilight. Some went straight to their own rooms, where they would smoke tobacco—an old habit allowed by the College on account of its soothing and sedative influence—before going to bed. By ten o'clock everybody would be in bed and asleep. What more beautiful proof of the advance of Science than the fact that the whole of the twenty-four thousand people who formed the population of Canterbury dropped off to sleep the moment they laid their heads upon the pillow? This it is to have learned the proper quantities and kinds of food; the proper amount of bodily exercise and work; and the complete subjugation of all the ancient forces of unrest and disquiet. To be sure, we were all, with one or two exceptions, in the very prime and flower of early manhood and womanhood. It would be hard, indeed, if a young man of thirty should not sleep well.

I was presently joined in the garden of the College by the Arch Physician.

"Grout," he said, "let us sit and talk. My mind is disturbed. It is always disturbed when the memory of the Past is forced upon me."

"The Evil Past," I said.

"If you please—the Evil Past. The question is, whether it was not infinitely more tolerable for mankind than the Evil Present?"

We argued out the point; but it was one on which we could never agree, for he remained saturated with the old ideas of private property and individualism. He maintained that there are no Rights of Man at all, except his Right to what he can get and what he can keep. He even went so far as to say that the true use of the Great Discovery should have been to cause the incompetent, the idle, the hereditarily corrupt, and the vicious to die painlessly.

"As to those who were left," he said, "I would have taught them the selfishness of staying too long. When they had taken time for work and play and society and love, they should have been exhorted to go away of their own accord, and to make room for their children. Then we should have had always the due succession of father and son, mother and daughter; always age and manhood and childhood; and always the world advancing by the efforts of those who would have time to work for an appreciable period. Instead, we have"—he waved his hand.

I was going to reply, when suddenly a voice light, clear, and sweet broke upon our astonished ears. 'Twas the voice of a woman, and she was singing. At first I hardly listened, because I knew that it could be none other than the child Christine, whom, indeed, I had often heard singing. It is natural, I believe, for children to sing. But the Arch Physician listened, first with wonder, and then with every sign of amazement. How could he be concerned by the voice of a child singing silly verses? Then I heard the last lines of her song, which she sang, I admit, with great vigor:

> *"Oh, Love is worth the whole broad earth;*
> *Oh, Love is worth the whole broad earth;*
> *Give that, you give us all!"*

"Grout," cried the Arch Physician, in tones of the deepest agitation, "I choke—I am stifled. Listen! They are words that I wrote—I myself wrote—with my own hand—long, long ago in the Past. I wrote them for a girl—the girl I told you of at dinner. I loved her. I thought never again to feel as I felt then. Yet the memory of that feeling has come back to me. Is it possible? Can some things never die? Can we administer no drug that will destroy memory? For the earth reeled beneath my feet again, and my senses reeled, and I would once more—yes, I would once more have given all the world—yes, life—even life—only to call that woman mine for a year—a month—a day—an hour!"

The Arch Physician made this astonishing confession in a broken and agitated voice. Then he rushed away, and left me alone in the summer-house.

The singer could certainly have been none other than the girl Christine. How should she get hold of Dr. Linister's love-song? Strange! She had disturbed our peace at supper by laughing, and she had agitated the Arch Physician himself to such a degree as I should have believed impossible by singing a foolish old song. When I went to bed there came into my mind some of the old idle talk about witches, and I even dreamed that we were burning a witch who was filling our minds with disturbing thoughts.

III

CHRISTINE AT HOME

When the girl Christine walked through the loitering crowd outside the Hall, some of the people looked after her with wondering eyes.

"Strange!" said a woman. "She laughed! She laughed!"

"Ay," said another, "we have forgotten how to laugh. But we used to laugh before"—she broke off with a sigh.

"And she sings," said a third. "I have heard her sing like a lark in the Museum."

"Once," said the first woman, "we used to sing as well as laugh. I remember, we used to sing. She makes us remember the old days."

"The bad old days"—it was one of the Assistant Physicians who admonished her—"the times when nothing was certain, not even life, from day to day. It should bring you increased happiness to think sometimes of those old times."

The first woman who had spoken was one whom men would have called beautiful in those old times, when their heads were turned by such a thing as a woman's face. She was pale of cheek and had black eyes, which, in those days of passion and jealousy, might have flashed like lightning. Now they were dull. She was shapely of limb and figure too, with an ample cheek and a full mouth. Formerly, in the days of love and rage, those limbs would have been lithe and active; now they were heavy and slow. Heaviness of movement and of eyes sensibly grows upon our people. I welcome every indication of advance towards the Perfect Type of Humanity which will do nothing but lie down, breathe, eat, and sleep.

"Yes," she replied with a deep sigh. "Nothing was certain. The bad old times, when people died. But there was love, and we danced and sung and laughed." She sighed again, and walked away alone, slowly, hanging her head.

The girl passed through them, leading the old man by the hand.

I know very well, now, that we ought to have been suspicious. What meant the gleam and sparkle of her eyes, when all other eyes were dull? What meant the parting of her lips and the smile which always lay upon them, when no one else smiled at all? Why did she carry her head erect, when the rest walked with hanging heads? Why, again, did she sing, when no one else sang? Why did she move as if her limbs were on springs, when all the rest went slowly and heavily? These signs meant mischief. I took them for the natural accompaniments of youth. They meant more than youth: they meant dangerous curiosity; they meant—presently—Purpose. How should one of the People dare to have a Purpose unknown to the Sacred College? You shall hear.

All that followed was, in fact, due to our own blindness. We should long before have shut up every avenue which might lead the curious to the study of the Past; we should have closed the Museum and the Library altogether. We did not, because we lived in the supposition that the more the old times were investigated, the more the people would be satisfied with the Present. When, indeed, one looks at the pictures of battle, murder, cruelty, and all kinds of passion; when one reads the old books, full of foolishness which can only be excused on the plea of a life too short to have a right comprehension of anything, it is amazing that the scene does not strike the observer with a kind of horror. When, which is seldom, I carry my own memory back to the old times and see myself before I went to the Laboratory, boy-of-all-work to a Brewery, ordered here and there, working all day long with no other prospect than to be a servant for a short span of life and then to die; when I remember the people among whom I lived, poor, starving, dependent from day to day on the chance of work, or, at best, from week to week; when I think of the misery from which these poor people have been rescued, I cannot find within me a spark of sympathy for the misguided wretches who voluntarily exchanged their calm and happy Present for the tumult and anxiety of the Past. However, we are not all reasonable, as you shall hear.

It was already twilight outside, and in the Museum there was only light enough to see that a few persons were assembled in the Great Hall. Christine placed her grandfather in a high-backed wooden chair, in which he spent most of his time, clutching at the arms and fighting with his asthma. Then she turned up the electric light. It showed a large, rather lofty room, oblong in shape. Old arms were arranged round the walls; great glass-cases stood about, filled with a collection of all kinds of things preserved from the old times. There were illustrations of their arts, now entirely useless: such as the jewels they wore, set in bracelets and necklaces; their gloves, fans, rings, umbrellas, pictures, and statuary.

Then there were cases filled with the old implements of writing—paper, inkstands, pens, and so forth—the people have long since left off writing; there were boxes full of coins with which they bought things, and for which they sold their freedom; there were things with which they played games—many of them dangerous ones—and whiled away the tedium of their short lives; there were models of the ships in which they went to sea, also models of all kinds of engines and machines which slaves—they were nearly all slaves—made for the purpose of getting more money for their masters; there were also crowns, coronets, and mitres, which formerly belonged to people who possessed what they called rank; there were the praying-books which were formerly used every day in great buildings like the House of Life; there were specimens of legal documents on parchment, by the drawing up of which, when law existed, a great many people procured a contemptible existence; there were also models, with figures of the people in them, of Parliament Houses, Churches, and Courts of Justice; there were life-size models of soldiers in uniform, when men were of understanding so contemptible as to be tempted to risk life—even life—in exchange for a gold-laced coat! But then our ancestors were indescribably foolish. There were musical instruments of all kinds—I have always been glad that music fell so soon into disuse. It is impossible to cultivate contentment while music is practised. Besides the ordinary weapons—sword, pike, and javelin—there were all kinds of horrible inventions, such as vast cannons, torpedo boats, dynamite shells, and so forth, for the destruction of towns, ships, and armor. It is a great and splendid Collection, but it ought to have been long, long before transferred to the custody of the Holy College.

The girl looked inquiringly at her visitors, counting them all. There were ten—namely, five men and five women. Like all the people, they were young—the men about thirty, the women about twenty-two or twenty-three. The men were dressed in their blue flannels, with a flat cap of the same material; the women in their gray beige, short frock, the flat gray cap under which their hair was gathered, gray stockings, and heavy shoes. The dress was, in fact, invented by myself for both sexes. It has many advantages. First, there is always plenty of the stuff to be had; next, both flannel and beige are soft, warm, and healthy textures—with such a dress there is no possibility of distinction or of superiority; and, lastly, with such a dress the women have lost all power of setting forth their attractions so as to charm the men with new fashions, crafty subtleties of dress, provocations of the troublesome passion of love in the shape of jewels, ribbons, gloves, and the like. No one wears gloves: all the women's hands are hard; and although they are still young and their faces are unchanged, their eyes are dull and hard. I am pleased to think that there is no more foolishness of love among us.

The people were standing or sitting about, not together, but separately—each by himself or herself. This tendency to solitary habits is a most healthy indication of the advance of humanity. Self-preservation is the first Law—separate and solitary existence is the last condition—of mankind. They were silent and regardless of each other. Their attitude showed the listlessness of their minds.

"I am glad you are here," said Christine. "You promised you would not fail me. And yet, though you promised, I feared that at the last moment you might change your mind. I was afraid that you would rather not be disturbed in the even current of your thoughts."

"Why disturb our minds?" asked one, a woman. "We were at peace before you began to talk of the Past. We had almost forgotten it. And it is so long ago"—her voice sank to a murmur—"so long ago."

They all echoed,

"It is so long ago—so long ago!"

"Oh," cried the girl, "you call this to be at peace! Why, if you were so many stones in the garden you could not be more truly at peace. To work, to rest, to eat, to sleep—you call that Life! And yet you can remember—if you please—the time when you were full of activity and hope."

"If to remember is to regret, why should we invite the pain of regret? We cannot have the old life except with the old conditions; the short life and the—"

"If I could remember—if I had ever belonged to the Past," the girl interrupted, quickly; "oh, I would remember every moment—I would live every day of the old life over and over again. But I can do nothing—nothing—but read of the splendid Past and look forward to such a future as your own. Alas! why was I born at all, since I was born into such a world as this? Why was I called into existence when all the things of which I read every day have passed away? And what remains in their place?"

"We have Life," said one of the men, but not confidently.

"Life! Yes—and what a life! Oh, what a life! Well, we waste time. Listen now—and if you can, for once forget the present and recall the past. Do not stay to think how great a gulf lies between; do not count the years—indeed, you cannot. Whether they are one hundred or five hundred they do not know, even at the Holy College itself. I am sure it will make you happier—'twill console and comfort you—in this our life of desperate monotony, only to remember—to recall—how you used to live."

They answered with a look of blank bewilderment.

"It is so long ago—so long ago," said one of them again.

"Look around you. Here are all the things that used to be your own. Let them help you to remember. Here are the arms that the men carried when they went out to fight; here are the jewels that the women wore. Think of your dress in the days when you were allowed to dress, and we did not all wear frocks of gray beige, as if all women were exactly alike. Will that not help?"

They looked about them helplessly. No, they did not yet remember; their dull eyes were filled with a kind of anxious wonder, as might be seen in one rudely awakened out of sleep. They looked at the things in the great room, but that seemed to bring nothing back to their minds. The Present was round them like a net which they could neither cut through nor see through; it was a veil around them through which they could not pass. It had been so long with them; it was so unchanging; for so long they had had nothing to expect; for so long, therefore, they had not cared to look back. The Holy College had produced, in fact, what it had proposed and designed. The minds of the people had become quiescent. And to think that so beautiful a state of things should be destroyed by a girl—the only child in the Community!

"Will it help," said the girl, "if we turn down the light a little? So. Now we are almost in darkness, but for the moonlight through the window. In the old times, when you were children, I have read that you loved to sit together and to tell stories. Let us tell each other stories."

Nobody replied; but the young man called Jack took Christine's hand and held it.

"Let us try," said the girl again. "I will tell you a story. Long ago there were people called gentlefolk. Grandad here was a gentleman. I have read about them in the old books. I wonder if any of you remember those people. They were exempt from work; the lower sort worked for them; they led a life of ease; they made their own work for themselves. Some of the men fought for their country—it was in the old time, you know, when men still fought; some worked for their country; some worked for the welfare of those who worked for bread; some only amused themselves; some were profligates, and did wicked things—"

She paused—no one responded.

"The women had no work to do at all. They only occupied themselves in making everybody happy; they were treated with the greatest respect; they were not allowed to do anything at all that could be done for them; they played and sang; they painted and embroidered; they knew foreign languages; they constantly inspired the men to do great things, even if they should be killed."

Here all shuddered and trembled. Christine made haste to change the subject.

"They wore beautiful dresses—think—dresses of silk and satin, embroidered with gold, trimmed with lace; they had necklaces, bracelets, and rings; their hands were white, and they wore long gloves to their elbows; they dressed their hair as they pleased. Some wore it long, like this." She pulled off her flat cap, and threw back her long tresses, and quickly turned up the light. She was transformed! The women started and gasped. "Take off your caps!" she ordered. They obeyed, and at sight of the flowing locks that fell upon their shoulders, curling, rippling, flowing, their eyes brightened, but only for a moment.

"Yes," said the girl, "they wore their beautiful hair as they pleased. Oh!"—she gathered in her hands the flowing tresses of one—"you have such long and beautiful hair! It is a shame—it is a shame to hide it. Think of the lovely dresses to match this beauty of the hair!"

"Oh," cried the women, "we remember the dresses. We remember them now. Why make us remember them? It is so long ago—so long ago—and we can never wear them any more."

"Nay; but you have the same beauty," said Christine. "That at least remains. You have preserved your youth and your beauty."

"Of what good are our faces to us," said another woman, "with such a dress as this? Men no longer look upon our beauty."

"Let us be," said the woman who had spoken first. "There can be no change for us. Why disturb our minds? The Present is horrible. But we have ceased to care much for anything: we do our day's work every day— all the same hours of work; we wear the same dress—to every woman the same dress; we eat and drink the same food—to every one the same; we are happy because we have got all we can get, and we expect no more; we never talk—why should we talk? When you laughed to-day it was like an earthquake." Her words were strong, but her manner of speech was a monotone. This way of speaking grows upon us; it is the easiest. I watch the indications with interest. From rapid talk to slow talk; from animated talk to monotony; the next step will be to silence absolute. "There is no change for us," she repeated, "neither in summer nor in winter. We have preserved our youth, but we have lost all the things which the youthful used to desire. We thought to preserve our beauty; what is the good of beauty with such a dress and such a life? Why should we make ourselves miserable in remembering any of the things we used to desire?"

"Oh," cried the girl, clasping her hands, "to me there is no pleasure possible but in learning all about the Past. I read the old books, I look at the old pictures, I play the old music, I sing the old songs; but it is not enough. I know how you were dressed—not all alike in gray beige frocks, but in lovely silk and beautiful embroidered stuffs. I will show you presently how you dressed. I know how you danced and played games and acted most beautiful plays, and I have read stories about you; I know that you were always dissatisfied, and wanting something or other. The stories are full of discontent; nobody ever sits down satisfied except one pair. There is always one pair, and they fall in Love—in Love," she repeated. "What is that, I wonder?" Then she went on again: "They only want one thing then, and the story-books are all about how they got it after wonderful adventures. There are no adventures now. The books tell us all this, but I want more. I want to know more: I want to see the old stories with my own eyes; I want to see you in your old dresses, talking in your own old way. The books cannot tell me how you talked and how you looked. I am sure it was not as you talk now—because you never talk."

"There is no reason why we should talk. All the old desires have ceased to be. We no longer want anything or expect anything."

"Come. I shall do my best to bring the Past back to you. First, I have learned who you were. That is why I have called you together. In the old times you all belonged to gentlefolk."

This announcement produced no effect at all. They listened with lack-lustre looks. They had entirely forgotten that there were ever such distinctions as gentle and simple.

"You will remember presently," said Christine, not discouraged. "I have found out in the ancient Rolls your names and your families."

"Names and families," said one of the men, "are gone long ago. Christine, what is the good of reviving the memory of things that can never be restored?"

But the man named Jack Carera, the sailor of whom I have already spoken, stepped forward. I have said that the sailors were a dangerous class, on account of their independence and their good meaning.

"Tell us," he said, "about our families. Why, I, for one, have never forgotten that I was once a gentleman. It is hard to tell now, because they have made us all alike; but for many, many years—I know not how many—we who had been gentlemen consorted together."

"You shall again," said Christine, "if you please. Listen, then. First, my grandfather. He was called Sir Arthur Farrance, and he was called a Baronet. To be a Baronet was, in those days, something greatly desired by many people. A man, in the old books, was said to enjoy the title of Baronet. But I know not why one man was so raised above another."

"Heugh! Heugh! Heugh!" coughed the old man. "I remember that. Why, what is there to remember except the old times? I was a Baronet— the fifth Baronet. My country place was in Sussex, and my town address was White's and the Travellers'."

"Yes," Christine nodded. "My grandfather's memory is tenacious; he forgets nothing of the things that happened when he was young. I have learned a great deal from him. He seems to have known all your grandmothers, for instance, and speaks of them as if he had loved them all."

"I did—I did," said the old man. "I loved them every one."

The girl turned to the women before her—the dull-eyed, heavy-headed women, all in the gray dresses exactly alike; but their gray flat caps had been thrown off, and they looked disturbed, moved out of the common languor.

"Now I will tell you who you were formerly. You"—she pointed to the nearest—"were the Lady Mildred Carera, only daughter of the Earl of Thordisá. Your father and mother survived the Discovery, but were killed in the Great Massacre Year, when nearly all the old were put to death. You were a great beauty in your time, and when the Discovery was announced you were in your second season. People wondered who would win you. But those who pretended to know talked of a young scientific Professor."

The woman heard as if she was trying to understand a foreign language. This was, in fact, a language without meaning to her. As yet she caught nothing.

"You," said Christine, turning to the next, "were Dorothy Oliphant; you were also young, beautiful, and an heiress; you, like Lady Mildred, had all the men at your feet. I don't know what that means, but the books say so. Then the Discovery came, and love-making, whatever that was, seems to have gone out of fashion." The second woman heard this information with lack-lustre eyes. What did it matter?

"You"—Christine turned to a third and to a fourth and fifth—"you were Rosie Lorrayne; you, Adela Dupré; you, Susie Campbell. You were all in Society; you were all young and beautiful and happy. Now for the men." She turned to them. The sailor named Jack gazed upon her with eyes of admiration. The other men, startled at first by the apparition of the tresses, had relapsed into listlessness. They hardly looked up as she addressed them.

First she pointed to the sailor.

"Your name—"

"I remember my name," he said. "I have not forgotten so much as our friends. Sailors talk more with each other, and remember. I am named John Carera, and I was formerly first-cousin to Lady Mildred. Cousin"—he held out his hand—"have you forgotten your cousin? We used to play together in the old times. You promised to marry me when you should grow up."

Lady Mildred gave him her hand.

"It is so long ago—so long ago," she murmured; but her eyes were troubled. She had begun to remember the things put away and forgotten for so long.

"You"—Christine turned to another—"were Geoffrey Heron. You were Captain in a Cavalry Regiment. You will remember that presently, and a great deal more. You"—she turned to another—"were Laurence de Heyn, and you were a young Lawyer, intending to be a Judge. You will remember that, in time. You"—she turned to another—"were Jack Culliford; and you were a Private Secretary, intending to go into Parliament, and to rise perhaps to be Prime Minister. And you"—she turned to the last—"were Arnold Buckland, already a Poet of Society. You will all remember these things before long. Lastly, you all belonged to the people who were born rich, and never used to have any care or anxiety about their daily bread. Nor did you ever do any work, unless you chose."

"It is so long ago," said Lady Mildred—her face was brighter now—"that we have forgotten even that there ever were gentlefolk."

"It is not strange," said Christine, "that you should have forgotten it. Why should you remember anything? We are only a herd, one with another; one not greater, and one not less, than another. Now that you know your names again and remember clearly, because I have told you"—she repeated the information for fear they should again forget—"who and what you were, each of you—you will go on to remember more."

"Oh, what good? What good?" asked Lady Mildred.

"Because it will rouse you from your lethargy," said the girl, impetuously. "Oh, you sit in silence day after day; you walk alone; you ought to be together as you used to be, talking, playing. See! I have read the books; your lives were full of excitement. It makes my heart beat only to read how the men went out to fight, daring everything, for the sake of the women they loved."

"The men love us no longer," said Lady Mildred.

"If the brave men fell—" But here all faces, except the sailor's, turned pale, and they shuddered. Christine did not finish the sentence. She, too, shuddered.

In the old times I remember how, being then errand-boy in the Brewery, I used to listen, in the Whitechapel Road, to the men who, every Sunday morning and evening, used to tell us that religion was a mockery and a snare, invented by the so-called priests for their own selfish ends, so that they might be kept in sloth and at their ease. There was no need now for these orators. The old religion was clean dead and forgotten. When men ceased to expect Death, what need was there to keep up any interest in the future world, if there should be any? But the bare mention of the dreadful thing is still enough to make all cheeks turn pale. Every year, the farther off Death recedes, the more terrible he looks. Therefore they all shuddered.

Among the musical instruments in the Museum there stands one, a square wooden box on legs, with wires inside it. There are many other musical instruments, the use of all (as I thought) forgotten. Very soon after the Great Discovery people ceased to care for music. For my own part, I have never been able to understand how the touching of chords and the striking of hammers on wires can produce any effect at all upon the mind except that of irritation. We preserve trumpets for the processions of the College because mere noise awes people, and because trumpets make more noise with less trouble than the human voice. But with music, such as it used to be, we have now nothing to do at all. I have been told that people were formerly greatly moved by music, so that every kind of emotion was produced in their minds merely by listening to a man or woman playing some instrument. It must have been so, because Christine, merely by playing the old music to the company, was able to bring back their minds to the long-forgotten Past. But it must be remembered that she had disturbed their minds first.

She sat down, then, before this box, and she began to play upon it, watching the people meanwhile. She played the music of their own time—indeed, there has been none written since. It was a kind of witchery. First the sailor named Jack sprang to his feet and began to walk up and down the room with wild gestures and strange looks. Then the rest, one by one, grew restless; they looked about them; they left their chairs and began to look at each other, and at the things in the cases. The Past was coming slowly into sight. I have heard how men at sea perceive an island far away, but like a cloud on the horizon; how the cloud grows larger and assumes outline; how this grows clearer and larger still, until, before the ship reaches the harbor and drops her anchor, the cliffs and the woods, and even the single trees on the hillsides, are clearly visible.

Thus the listeners gradually began to see the Past again. Now, to feel these old times again, one must go back to them and become once more part of them. It is possible, because we are still of the age when we left them. Therefore, this little company, who had left the old time when they were still young, began to look again as they had then looked. Their eyes brightened, their cheeks flushed; their limbs became elastic; their heads were thrown back; the faces of the women grew soft, and those of the men strong; on all alike there fell once more the look of restless expectancy and of unsatisfied yearning which belonged to all ages in the old time.

Presently they began to murmur, I know not what, and then to whisper to each other with gentle sighs. Then the girls—they were really girls again—caught each other by the hand, and panted and sighed again; and at last they fell upon each other's necks and kissed. As for the men, they now stood erect and firm, but for the most part they gazed upon the girls with wonder and admiration unspeakable, so great was the power of witchery possessed by this insignificant girl.

Christine looked on and laughed gently. Then she suddenly changed her music, and began to play a March loud and triumphant. And as she played she spoke:

"When the brave soldiers came home from battle and from victory, it was right that the people should all go forth to meet them. The music played for them; the children strewed roses under their feet; the bells were set ringing; the crowds cheered them; the women wept and laughed at the same time, and waved them welcome. Nothing could be too good for the men who fought for their country. Listen! I found the song of the Victors' Return in an old book. I wonder if you remember it. I think it is a very simple little thing."

Then she sang. She had a strong, clear voice—they had heard her singing before—no one sang in the whole City except this child, and already it had been observed that her singing made men restless. I do not deny the fulness and richness of her voice; but the words she sang— Dr. Linister's words, they were—are mere foolishness:

> "With flying flag, with beat of drum,
> Oh, brave and gallant show!
> In rags and tatters home they come—
> We love them better so.
> With sunburnt cheeks and wounds and scars;
> Yet still their swords are bright.
> Oh, welcome, welcome from the wars,
> Brave lads who fought the fight!

> "The girls they laugh, the girls they cry,
> 'What shall their guerdon be?—
> Alas! that some must fall and die!—
> Bring forth our gauds to see.
> 'Twere all too slight, give what we might,'
> Up spoke a soldier tall:
> 'Oh, Love is worth the whole broad earth;
> Oh, Love is worth the whole broad earth;
> Give that, you give us all!'"

"Do you remember the song?" Christine asked.

They shook their heads. Yet it seemed familiar. They remembered some such songs.

"Geoffrey Heron," said the girl, turning to one of the men, "you were Captain Heron in the old days. You remember that you were in the army."

"Was I?" He started. "No; yes. I remember. I was Captain Heron. We rode out of Portsmouth Dockyard Gates when we came home— all that were left of us. The women were waiting on the Hard outside, and they laughed and cried, and caught our hands, and ran beside the horses. Our ranks were thin, for we had been pretty well knocked about. I remember now. Yes—yes, I was—I was Captain Heron."

"Go into that room. You will find your old uniform. Take off the blue flannels, and show us how you looked when you were in uniform."

As if it was nothing at all unusual, the man rose and obeyed. It was observed that he now carried himself differently. He stood erect, with shoulders squared, head up, and limbs straight. They all obeyed whatever this girl ordered them to do.

Christine began to play again. She played another March, but always loud and triumphant.

When the soldier came back he was dressed in the uniform which he had worn in the time of the Great Discovery, when they left off taking account of time.

"Oh!" cried Christine, springing to her feet. "See! See! Here is a soldier! Here is a man who has fought!"

He stood before them dressed in a scarlet tunic and a white helmet; a red sash hung across him, and on his breast were medals. At sight of him the girl called Dorothy Oliphant changed countenance; all caught their breath. The aspect of the man carried them, indeed, back to the old, old time.

"Welcome home, Captain Heron," said Christine. "We have followed your campaign day by day."

"We are home again," the soldier replied, gravely. "Unfortunately, we have left a good many of our regiment behind."

"Behind? You mean—they—are—dead." Christine shuddered. The others shuddered. Even Captain Heron himself for a moment turned pale. But he was again in the Past, and the honor of his regiment was in his hands.

"You have fought with other men," said Christine. "Let me look in your face. Yes—it is changed. You have the look of the fighting man in the old pictures. You look as if you mean to have something, whatever it is, whether other men want it or not. Oh, you have fought with men! It is wonderful! Perhaps you have even killed men. Were you dreadfully afraid?"

Captain Heron started and flushed.

"Afraid?" he asked. "Afraid?"

"Oh!" Christine clapped her hands. "I wanted to see that look. It is the look of a man in sudden wrath. Forgive me! It is terrible to see a man thus moved. No, Captain Heron, no! I understand. An officer in your regiment could be afraid of nothing."

She sat down, still looking at him.

"I have seen a soldier," she said. Then she sprang to her feet. "Now," she cried, "it is our turn. Come with me, you ladies; and you, gentlemen, go into that room. For one night we will put on the dresses you used to wear. Come!"

They obeyed. There was nothing that they would not have done, so completely had she bewitched them. How long since they had been addressed as ladies and gentlemen!

"Come," she said, in the room whither she led the women, "look about, and choose what you please. But we must make haste."

There was a great pile of dainty dresses laid out for them to choose—dresses in silk and all kinds of delicate stuffs, with embroidery, lace, ribbons, jewels, chains, rings, bracelets, gloves, fans, shoes—everything that the folly of the past time required to make rich women seem as if they were not the same as their poorer sisters.

They turned over the dresses, and cried out with admiration. Then they hastened to tear off their ugly gray frocks, and began to dress.

But the girl called Dorothy Oliphant sank into a chair. "Oh, he has forgotten me! he has forgotten me! Who am I that he should remember me after all these years?"

"Why," said Christine, "how should he remember? What matters that you have the same face? Think of your dull look and your heavy eyes; think of the dowdy dress and the ugly cap. Wait till you have put on a pretty frock and have dressed your hair; here is a chain of pearls which will look pretty in your hair; here is a sweet colored silk. I am sure it will fit you. Oh, it is a shame—it is a shame that we have to dress so! Never mind. Now I have found out the old dresses, we will have many evenings together. We will go back to the Past. He will remember you, Dorothy dear. Oh, how could you give them up? How *could* you give up your lovely dresses?"

"We were made to give them up because there were not enough beautiful dresses to go round. They said that no woman must be dressed better than another. So they invented—it was Dr. Grout, the Suffragan, who did it—the gray dress for the women and the blue flannel for the men. And I had almost forgotten that there were such things. Christine, my head is swimming. My heart is beating. I have not felt my heart beating for I know not how long. Oh, will Geoffrey remember me when I am dressed?"

"Quick! Of course he will. Let me dress you. Oh, I often come here in the daytime and dress up, and pretend that it is the Past again. You shall come with me. But I want to hear you talk as you used to talk, and to see you dance as you used to dance. Then I shall understand it all."

When they returned, the men were waiting for them. Their blue flannels were exchanged for black cloth clothes, which it had been the custom of those who called themselves gentlemen to wear in the evening. In ancient times this was their absurd custom, kept up in order to mark the difference between a gentleman and one of the lower class. If you had no dress-coat, you were not a gentleman. How could men ever tolerate, for a single day, the existence of such a social difference? As for me, in the part of London where I lived, called Whitechapel, there were no dress-coats. The change, however, seemed to have transformed them. Their faces had an eager look, as if they wanted something. Of course, in the old times everybody always wanted something. You can see it in the pictures—the faces are never at rest; in the portraits, the eyes are always seeking for something; nowhere is there visible the least sign of contentment. These unfortunate men had acquired, with their old clothes, something of the old restlessness.

Christine laughed aloud and clapped her hands.

The women did not laugh. They saluted the men, who bowed with a certain coldness. The manners of the Past were coming back to them swiftly, but the old ease was not recovered for the first quarter of an hour. Then Captain Heron, who had changed his uniform for civilian dress, suddenly flushed and stepped forward, whispering,

"Dorothy, you have forgotten me?"

Dorothy smiled softly, and gave him her hand with a quick sigh. No, she had not forgotten him.

"Dance!" said Christine. "I want to see you dance. I will play for you."

She played a piece of music called a Waltz. When this kind of music used to be played—I mean in the houses of (so-called) ladies, not those of the People—the young men and women caught each other round the waist and twirled round. They had many foolish customs, but none more foolish, I should suppose, than this. I have never seen the thing done, because all this foolishness was forgotten as soon as we settled down to the enjoyment of the Great Discovery. When, therefore, Christine began this music, they looked at each other for a few moments, and then, inspired by memory, they fell into each other's arms and began their dance.

She played for them for a quarter of an hour. While the rest danced, the young man Jack stood beside the piano, as if he was chained to the spot. She had bewitched them all, but none so much as this man. He therefore gazed upon the girl with an admiration which certainly belonged to the old time. Indeed, I have never been able to understand how the Past could be so suddenly assumed. To admire—actually to admire—a woman, knowing all the time—it is impossible to conceal the fact—that she is your inferior, that she is inferior in strength and intellect! Well, I have already called them unfortunate men; I can say no more. How can people admire things below themselves? When she had played for a quarter of an hour or so, this young man called upon her to stop. The dancers stopped too, panting, their eyes full of light, their cheeks flushed and their lips parted.

"Oh," Dorothy sighed, "I never thought to feel such happiness again. I could dance on forever."

"With me?" murmured Geoffrey. "I was praying that the last round might never stop. With me?"

"With you," she whispered.

"Come!" cried the young man Jack. "It is too bad. Christine must dance. Play for us, Cousin Mildred, and I will give her a lesson."

Mildred laughed. Then she started at the unwonted sound. The others laughed to hear it, and the walls of the Museum echoed with the laughter of girls. The old man sat up in his chair and looked around.

"I thought I was at Philippe's, in Paris," he said. "I thought we were having a supper after the theatre. There was Ninette, and there was Madeleine—and—and—"

He looked about him bewildered. Then he dropped his head and went to sleep again. When he was neither eating nor battling for his breath, he was always sleeping.

"I am your cousin, Jack," said Mildred; "but I had long forgotten it. And as for playing—but I will try. Perhaps the old touch will return."

It did. She played with far greater skill and power than the self-taught Christine, but not (as they have said since) with greater sweetness.

Then Jack took Christine and gave her a first lesson. It lasted nearly half an hour.

"Oh," cried the girl, when Lady Mildred stopped, "I feel as if I had been floating round in a dream. Was I a stupid pupil, Jack?"

"You were the aptest pupil that dancing-master ever had."

"I know now," she said, with panting breath and flushed cheeks, "what dancing means. It is wonderful that the feet should answer to the music. Surely you must have loved dancing?"

"We did," the girls replied; "we did. There was no greater pleasure in the world."

"Why did you give it up?"

They looked at each other.

"After the Great Discovery," said Dorothy Oliphant, "we were so happy to get rid of the terrors of old age, and the loss of our beauty, and everything, that at first we thought of nothing else. When we tried to dance again, something had gone out of it. The men were not the same. Perhaps we were not the same. Everything languished after that. There was no longer any enjoyment. We ceased to dance because we found no pleasure in dancing."

"But now you do?" said Christine.

"To-night we do, because you have filled our hearts with the old thoughts. To get out of the dull, dull round—why is it that we never felt it dull till to-night? Oh, so long as we can remember the old thoughts, let us continue to dance and to play and to sing. If the old thoughts cease to come back to us"—she looked at Geoffrey—"let us fall back into our dulness, like the men and women round us."

"It was to please me first," said Christine. "You were so very kind as to come here to please me, because I can have no recollection at all of the Past, and I was curious to understand what I read. Come again—to please yourselves. Oh, I have learned so much—so very much more than I ever expected! There are so many, many things that I did not dream of. But let us always dance," she said—"let us always dance—let me always feel every time you come as if there was nothing in the world but sweet music calling me, and I was spinning round and round, but always in some place far better and sweeter than this."

"Yes," Lady Mildred said, gravely. "Thus it was we used to feel."

"And I have seen you as you were—gentlemen and gentlewomen together. Oh, it is beautiful! Come every night. Let us never cease to change the dismal Present for the sunny Past. But there is one thing—one thing that I cannot understand."

"What is that?" asked Lady Mildred.

"In the old books there is always, as I said before, a young man in love with a girl. What is it—Love?" The girls sighed and cast down their eyes. "Was it possible for a man so to love a girl as to desire nothing in the world but to have her love, and even to throw away his life—actually his very life—his very life—for her sake?"

"Dorothy," said Geoffrey, taking both her hands, "was it possible? Oh, was it possible?"

Dorothy burst into tears.

"It *was* possible!" she cried; "but oh, it is not possible any longer."

"Let us pretend," said Geoffrey, "let us dream that it is possible."

"Even to throw away your life—to die—actually your life?" asked Christine. "To die? To exist no longer? To abandon life—for the sake of another person?"

A sudden change passed over all their faces. The light died out of their eyes; the smile died on their lips; the softness vanished from the ladies' faces; the men hung their heads. All their gallantry left them. And Geoffrey let Mildred's hands slip from his holding. The thought of Death brought them all back to the Present.

"No," said Lady Mildred, sadly, and with changed voice, "such things are no longer possible. Formerly, men despised death because it was certain to come, in a few years at best; and why not, therefore, to-morrow? But we cannot brave death any more. We live, each for himself. That is the only safety; there is only the law of self-preservation. All are alike; we cannot love each other any more, because we are all alike. No woman is better than another in any man's eyes, because we are all dressed the same, and we are all the same. What more do we want?" she said, harshly. "There is no change for us; we go from bed to work, from work to rest and food, and so to bed again. What more can we want? We are all equals; we are all the same; there are no more gentlewomen. Let us put on our gray frocks and our flat caps again, and hide our hair and go home to bed."

"Yes, yes," cried Christine, "but you will come again. You will come again, and we will make every night a Play and Pretence of the beautiful—the lovely Past. When we lay aside the gray frocks, and let down our hair, we shall go back to the old time—the dear old time."

The young man named Jack remained behind when the others were gone. "If it were possible," he said, "for a man to give up everything—even his life—for a woman, in the old times, when life was a rich and glorious possession—how much more ought he not to be willing to lay it down, now that it has been made a worthless weed?"

"I have never felt so happy"—the girl was thinking of something else. "I have never dreamed that I could feel so happy. Now I know what I have always longed for—to dance round and round forever, forgetting all but the joy of the music and the dance. But oh, Jack"—her face turned pale again—"how could they ever have been happy, even while they waltzed, knowing that every minute brought them nearer and nearer to the dreadful end?"

"I don't know. Christine, if I were you, I would never mention that ugly topic again, except when we are not dressed up and acting. How lovely they looked—all of them—but none of them to compare with the sweetest rose-bud of the garden?"

He took her hand and kissed it, and then left her alone with the old man in the great Museum.

IV

What is Love?

I t would be idle to dwell upon the repetition of such scenes as those described in the last chapter. These unhappy persons continued to meet day after day in the Museum; after changing their lawful garments for the fantastic habits worn before the Great Discovery, they lost themselves nightly in the imagination of the Past. They presently found others among the People, who had also been gentlewomen and gentlemen in the old days, and brought them also into the company; so that there were now, every evening, some thirty gathered together. Nay, they even procured food and made suppers for themselves, contrary to the practice of common meals enjoined by the Holy College; they gloried in being a company apart from the rest; and because they remembered the Past, they had the audacity to give themselves, but only among themselves, airs of superiority. In the daytime they wore the common dress, and were like the rest of the People. The thing grew, however. Every evening they recalled more of the long-vanished customs and modes of thought—one remembering this and the other that little detail—until almost every particular of the ancient life had returned to them. Then a strange thing happened. For though the Present offered still—and this they never denied—its calm, unchanging face, with no disasters to trouble and no certain and miserable end to dread; with no anxieties, cares, and miseries; with no ambitions and no struggles; they fell to yearning after the old things; they grew to loathe the Present; they could hardly sit with patience in the Public Hall; they went to their day's work with ill-concealed disgust. Yet, so apathetic had the people grown that nothing of this was observed; so careless and so unsuspicious were we ourselves that though the singing and playing grew louder and continued longer every evening, none of us suspected anything. Singing, in my ears, was no more than an unmeaning noise; that the girl in the Museum should sing and play seemed foolish, but then children are foolish—they like to make a great noise.

One afternoon—it was some weeks since this dangerous fooling began—the cause of the whole, the girl Christine, was in the Museum alone. She had a book in her hand, and was reading in it. First she read a few lines, and then paused and meditated a while. Then she read again, and laughed gently to herself. And then she read, and changed color. And again she read, and knitted her brows as one who considers but cannot understand.

The place was quite deserted, save for her grandfather, who sat in his great chair, propped up with pillows and fast asleep. He had passed a bad night with his miserable asthma; in the morning, as often happens with this disease, he found himself able to breathe again, and was now therefore taking a good spell of sleep. His long white hair fell down upon his shoulders, his wrinkled old cheek showed a thousand crows' feet and lines innumerable; he looked a very, very old man. Yet he was no more than seventy-five or so, in the language of the Past. He belonged formerly to those who lived upon the labor of others, and devoured their substance. Now, but for his asthma, which even the College cannot cure, he should have been as perfectly happy as the rest of the People. The sunshine which warmed his old limbs fell full upon his chair; so that he seemed, of all the rare and curious objects in that collection, the rarest and most curious. The old armor on the wall, the trophies of arms, the glass vases containing all the things of the past, were not so rare and curious as this old man—the only old man left among us. I daily, for my own part, contemplated the old man with a singular satisfaction. He was, I thought, a standing lesson to the People, one daily set before their eyes. Here was the sole surviving specimen of what in the Past was the best that the men and women could expect—namely, to be spared until the age of seventy-five, and then to linger on afflicted with miserable diseases and, slowly or swiftly, to be tortured to death. Beholding that spectacle, I argued, all the people ought to rub their hands in complacency and gratitude. But our people had long ceased to reason or reflect. The lesson was consequently thrown away upon them. Nay, when this girl began her destructive career, those whom she dragged into her toils only considered this old man because he would still be talking, as all old men used to talk, about the days of his youth, for the purpose of increasing their knowledge of the Past, and filling their foolish souls with yearning after the bad old times.

While Christine read and pondered, the door of the Museum opened. The young man called Jack stood there gazing upon her. She had thrown off her cap, and her long brown curls lay over her shoulders. She had a red rose in the bosom of her gray dress, and she had tied a crimson scarf round her waist. Jack (suffer me to use the foolishness of their language—of course his name was John)—closed the door silently.

"Christine," he whispered.

She started, and let her book fall. Then she gave him her hand, which he raised to his lips. (Again I must ask leave to report a great deal of foolishness.)

"It is the sweet old fashion," he said. "It is my homage to my lady."

They were now so far gone in folly that she accepted this act as if it was one natural and becoming.

"I have been reading," she said, "a book full of extracts—all about love. I have never understood what love is. If I ask Dorothy, she looks at Geoffrey Heron and sighs. If I ask him, he tells me that he cannot be my servant to teach me, because he is already sworn to another. What does this mean? Have the old times come back again, so that men once more call themselves slaves of love? Yet what does it mean?"

"Tell me," said Jack, "what you have been reading."

"Listen, then. Oh, it is the strangest extravagance! What did men mean when they could gravely write down, and expect to be read, such things as—

> *"I do love you more than words can wield the matter—*
> *Dearer than eyesight, space, and liberty;*
> *Beyond what can be valued, rich or rare?'*

'Dearer than eyesight, space, and liberty.' Did they really mean that?"

"They meant more; they meant dearer than life itself!" said Jack, slowly. "Only it was stupid always to say the same thing."

"Well, then, listen to this:

> *"Had I no eyes but ears, my ears would love*
> *That inward beauty and invisible;*
> *Or, were I deaf, thy outward parts would move*
> *Each part in me that were but sensible.*
> *Though neither eyes nor ears, to hear nor see,*
> *Yet should I be in love, by touching thee.'*

Now, Jack, what can that mean? Was anything more absurd?"

"Read another extract, Christine."

"Here is a passage more difficult than any other:

> *"'Love looks not with the eyes, but with the mind;*
> *And therefore is wing'd Cupid painted blind.*
> *Nor hath Love's mind of any judgment taste;*
> *Wings and no eyes, figure unheedy haste.*
> *And therefore is Love said to be a child,*
> *Because in choice he is so oft beguiled.'*

Tell me, if you can, what this means. But perhaps you were never in love, Jack, in the old times."

"Romeo was in love before he met Juliet," said Jack. "I, too, have been reading the old books, you see, Child. I remember—but how can I tell you? I cannot speak like the poet. Yet I remember—I remember." He looked round the room. "It is only here," he murmured, "that one can clearly remember. Here are the very things which used to surround our daily life. And here are youth and age. They were always with us in the old time—youth and age. Youth with love before, and age with love behind. Always we knew that as that old man, so should we become. The chief joys of life belonged to youth; we knew very well that unless we snatched them then we should never have them. To age we gave respect, because age, we thought, had wisdom; but to us—to us—who were young, age cried unceasingly—

> *"'Gather ye rose-buds while ye may.'*

If I could tell only you! Christine, come with me into the Picture Gallery. My words are weak, but the poets and the painters speak for us. Come! We shall find something there that will speak for me what I have not words to say for myself."

Nothing in the whole world—I have maintained this in the College over and over again—has done so much harm to Humanity as Art. In a world of common-sense which deals with nothing but fact and actuality, Art can have no place. Why imitate what we see around us? Artists cheated the world; they pretended to imitate, and they distorted or they exaggerated. They put a light into the sky that never was there; they filled the human face with yearning after things impossible; they put thoughts into the heart which had no business there; they made woman into a goddess, and made love—simple love—a form of worship; they exaggerated every joy; they created a heaven which could not exist. I have seen their pictures, and I know it. Why—why did we not destroy all works of Art long ago—or, at least, why did we not enclose the Gallery, with the Museum, within the College wall?

The Picture Gallery is a long room with ancient stone walls; statuary is arranged along the central line, and the pictures line the walls.

The young man led the girl into the Gallery and looked around him. Presently he stopped at a figure in white marble. It represented a woman, hands clasped, gazing upward. Anatomically, I must say, the figure is fairly correct.

"See," he said, "when in the olden times our sculptors desired to depict the Higher Life—which we have lost or thrown away for a while—they carved the marble image of a woman. Her form represented perfect beauty; her face represented perfect purity; the perfect soul must be wedded to the perfect body, otherwise there can be no perfection of Humanity. This is the Ideal Woman. Look in her face, look at the curves of her form, look at the carriage of her head; such a woman it was whom men used to love."

"But were women once like this? Could they look so? Had they such sweet and tender faces? This figure makes me ashamed."

"When men were in love, Christine, the woman that each man loved became in his mind such as this. He worshipped in his mistress the highest form of life that he could conceive. Some men were gross, their ideals were low; some were noble, then their ideals were high. Always there were among mankind some men who were continually trying to raise the ideal; always the mass of men were keeping the ideal low."

"Were the women ashamed to receive such worship? Because they must have known what they were in cold reality."

"Perhaps to the nobler sort," said the young man, "to be thought so good lifted up their hearts and kept them at that high level. But indeed I know not. Remember that when men wrote the words that you think extravagant, they were filled and wholly possessed with the image of the Perfect Woman. Nay, the nobler and stronger their nature, the more they were filled with that Vision. The deeper their love for any woman, the higher they placed her on the Altar of their worship."

"And if another man should try to take that woman from them—"

"They would kill that other man," said Jack, with a fierce gleam in his eye, which made the girl shudder. Yet she respected him for it.

"If another man should come between us now, Christine, I would— Nay, dear, forgive my rude words. What has jealousy to do with you?"

She dropped her eyes and blushed, and in all her limbs she trembled.

WALTER BESANT

This young man made her afraid. And yet—she knew not why—it made her happy, only to be afraid of him.

"Let us see some of the pictures," said Jack.

There were many hundreds of them. They represented I know not what; scenes of the old life in the old time. I dare say everything was there, with all the exaggerations which pleased the painters and cheated the senses of those who looked on. Fair women were painted fairer than women could ever be; their eyes were larger, softer, fuller of thought; their cheeks more tender, their limbs more comely.

There were battle scenes; the young man led the girl past them. There were scenes from history—kings laying down crowns, traitors receiving sentence, and so forth; he passed them by. There were groups of nymphs, portraits of fair women, groups of girls dancing, girls at play, girls laughing, girls bathing; he passed them by. Presently he stopped before three panels side by side, representing a simple allegory of the old time. In the first picture, two, a young man and a girl, walked hand-in-hand beside a stream. The water danced and rippled in the sunlight; behind them was an orchard full of blossom; flowers sprang up at their feet—the flowers of spring. And they walked hand-in-hand, gazing in each other's eyes. The second picture showed a man in middle-age returning home from work; beside him walked his boys; in the porch the mother sat with her daughters spinning at the wheel. The stream was now a full majestic river; the trees were loaded with fruit not yet ripe; the fields were covered with corn, green still, but waving with light and shade under the summer sky; in the distance, passing away, was a heavy thunder-cloud. In the third panel an old pair stood beside a great river, looking out upon the ocean. Again they were hand-in-hand. The sun was setting in great splendor across the sea; the reapers were carrying their harvest home with songs and dances. And the old people still gazed in each other's face, just as they had done fifty years ago.

"See, Christine!" said Jack. "In the first panel, this pair think of nothing but of each other. Presently they will have other thoughts. The stream beside which they wander is the Stream of Life. It widens as it goes. While they walk along its banks, the river grows broader and deeper. This means that as they grow older they grow wiser and learn more. So they go on continually, until they come to the mouth of the river, where it loses itself in the ocean of—what our friends tremble so much as to name. Tell me, is there terror, or doubt, or anxiety on their faces now that they have come to the end?"

"No; their faces are entirely happy."

"This you do not understand. Christine, if you were sure that in the end you would be as happy as that old woman at the end, would you be content to begin with the beginning? Would you play the part of that girl, and walk—with me—along the Stream of Life?"

He took her hand, but she made no reply, save that her eyes filled with tears. Presently she murmured,

"They are always happy—at the beginning and at the end. Did they know at the beginning that there would be an end?"

"They knew; everybody knew; the very children knew almost from infancy the great Law of Nature, that for everything there is the allotted end. They knew it."

"And yet they were always happy. I cannot understand it."

"We have destroyed that happiness," said the young man. "Love cannot exist when there is no longer end, or change, or anything to hope or fear—no mystery, nothing to hope or fear. What is a woman outside the Museum in the eyes of the College? She is only the half of humanity, subject to disease and requiring food at intervals. She no longer attracts men by the sacred mystery of her beauty. She is not even permitted any longer to make herself beautiful by her dress; nor is she allowed to create the feeling of mystery and the unknown by seclusion. She lives in the open, like the rest. We all live together; we know what each one says and thinks and does; nay, most of us have left off thinking and talking altogether."

But Christine was hardly listening; she could not understand this talk. She was looking at the pictures.

"Oh," she said, "they look so happy! There is such a beautiful contentment in their eyes! They love each other so, that they think of nothing but their love. They have forgotten the end."

"Nay, but look at the end."

"They are happy still, although the river flows into the Ocean. How can they be happy?"

"You shall learn more, Christine. You have seen enough to understand that the talk of the Physicians about the miseries of the old time is mischievous nonsense, with which they have fooled us into slavery."

"Oh, if they heard you—"

"Let them hear," he replied, sternly. "I hope, before long, we may make them hear. Christine, you can restore the old love by your own example. You alone have nothing to remember and nothing to unlearn.

As for the rest of us, we have old habits to forget and prejudices to overcome before we can get back to the Past."

Then he led her to another picture.

The scene was a green village church-yard, standing amid trees—yews and oaks—and round a gray old church. Six strong men bore a bier piled with flowers towards an open grave, newly dug. Beside the grave stood one in a white robe, carrying a book. Behind the bier followed, hand-in-hand, a weeping company of men, women, and children. But he who walked first wept not.

"Oh," cried Christine, "he is dead! He is dead!"

She burst into tears.

"Nay," said Jack; "it is the wife who is dead. The husband lives still. See, he follows with tottering step. His grandchild leads him as you lead your grandfather. And they are all weeping except him. Why does he alone not weep? He has been married for fifty years and more; all his life has been shared by the love and sympathy of the woman—the dead woman. She is dead, my dear"—he repeated these words, taking the girl's hands—"she is dead, and he sheds no tears. Why not? Look at his face. Is it unhappy? Tell me, Christine, do you read the sorrow of hopelessness in that old man's face?"

"No, no," she said. "He is grave, but he is not unhappy. Yet here is Death, with all the terrible things that we read of in the books—the deep pit, the body to be lowered in the grave—oh!"

She shuddered and turned her head.

"As I read his face," said Jack, "I see hope and consolation."

"Why is there a man in white?"

"I will tell you some time. Meanwhile, observe that the old man is happy, though his wife is dead, and though he knows that to-morrow his turn will come, and a grave will be dug for him beside his wife, and he also will be laid among the cold clay-clods, as cold, as senseless as them, there to lie while the great world rolls round and round. He knows this, I say, and yet he is not unhappy."

"What does it mean, Jack?"

"I will tell you—soon."

"We who are sailors," this young man continued, "are not like the rest of the world. We are always exposed to danger; we are not afraid to speak of Death; and though we have taken advantage (as we thought) of the Great Discovery, we have never forgotten the Past or the old ideas. We have to think for ourselves, which makes us independent. There is no Holy College on board ship, and no sacred Physician ventures his precious life upon a rolling deck. When we come ashore, we look round and see things. Then we go on board again and talk, in the night watches below the stars. I think the Holy College would be pleased if they could sometimes hear our talk. Christine, there is no happiness left in the world except among those whom the Great Discovery cannot save from the dangers of a storm. When you spoke to me my heart leaped up, because I saw what as yet you do not see. The others were too sluggish to remember, until you had dragged their thoughts into the old channels; but there was no need to drag me; for I remember always, and I only pretended until the others should come with me."

Christine heard only half of this, for she was looking at the picture of the village funeral again.

"Oh, how could men be happy with such an end before them?" she cried. "I cannot understand it. To be torn away, to be laid in a box, to be put away deep underground, there to lie forever—oh!" She trembled again. "And not to be unhappy!"

"Look round the room, Christine. Read the faces. Here are portraits of men and women. Some of them are eager, some are calm, more are unhappy for thinking of the end. Here is a battle-field; the dead and wounded are lying about the ground. Look at this troop of horsemen charging. Is there any terror in their faces? What do they care about the men who have fallen? Their duty is to fight. See here again. It is a dying girl. What do you read in her face? I see no fear, but a sweet joy of resignation. Here is a man led forth to execution. There is no fear in his face."

"I could never bear to be alone in this room, because Death is everywhere, and no one seems to regard it."

"Christine, did you never hear, by any chance, from your grandfather why people were not afraid?"

"No; he cannot bear to speak of such a thing. He trembles and shakes if it is even mentioned. They all do, except you."

"What does he tell you?"

"He talks of the time when he was young. It was long before the Great Discovery. Oh, he is very old. He was always going to feasts and dances. He had a great many friends, and some of them used to sing and dance in theatres. They were all very fond of suppers after the theatre, and there was a great deal of singing and laughing. They used to drive about in carriages, and they went to races. I do not understand, very well, the pleasure of his life."

WALTER BESANT

"Ah," said Jack, "he has forgotten the really important part of it."

They were at a part of the Gallery where there was a door of strong oak, studded with big square nails, under an arch of carved stone.

"Have you ever been into this place?" he asked.

"Once I went in. But there is a dreadful tomb in it, with carved skulls and the figure of a dead man. So I ran away."

"Come in with me. You shall not be frightened."

He turned the great iron handle, and pushed open the heavy door.

The room was lofty, with a pointed roof. It was lit by long narrow windows, filled with painted glass. There were seats of carved wood, with carved canopies on either side; there was the figure of a brass eagle, with a great book upon it; and under the three lights of the window at the end was a table covered with a cloth which hung in rags and tatters, and was covered with dust. It was, in fact, an ancient Chapel, shut up and suffered to fall into decay.

"This," said the young man, "is the Chapel where, in the old time, they came to worship. They also worshipped in the great place that is now the House of Life. But here some of them worshipped also, though with less splendor."

"Did they," asked the girl, "worship the Beautiful Woman of their dreams?"

"No, not the Beautiful Woman. They worshipped her outside. In this Chapel they worshipped the Maker of Perfect Man and Perfect Woman. Come in with me, and I will tell you something of what it meant."

It was two hours and more before they came out of the Chapel. The girl's eyes were full of tears, and tears lay upon his cheeks.

"My dear, my love," said Jack, "I have tried to show you how the old true love was nourished and sustained. It would not have lived but for the short duration of its life; it was the heritage of each generation, to be passed on unto the next. Only on one condition was it possible. It is a condition which you have been taught to believe horrible beyond the power of words. I have tried to show you that it was not horrible. My love, my sweet—fresh as the maidens who in the old time blossomed and flowered, and presently fulfilled that condition—the only woman among us who is young in heart, let us agree to love—we two—after the old fashion, under the old conditions. Do not shiver, dear. There is the old faith to sustain us. You shall go to sea with me. Perhaps we shall be cast away and drowned; perhaps we shall contract some unknown disease and die. We shall presently lie down to sleep, and awake again in each other's arms once more in a new life which we cannot now comprehend. Everything must have an end. Human life must have an end, or it becomes horrible, monstrous, selfish. The life beyond will be glorified beyond all our hopes, and beyond all our imagination. My dear, are you afraid?"

She laid her head upon his shoulder.

"Oh, Jack, with you I am afraid of nothing. I should not be afraid to die this very moment, if we died together. Is it really true? Can we love now as men loved women long ago? Oh, can you love me so? I am so weak and small a creature—so weak and foolish! I would die with you, Jack—both together, taking each other by the hand; and oh, if you were to die first, I could not live after. I must, then, die too. My head is swimming—my heart is beating—lay your arm about me. Oh, love, my love; I have never lived before. Oh, welcome Life, and welcome Death, so that we may never, never more be parted!"

V

The Open Door

It was in this way that the whole trouble began. There was an inquisitive girl foolishly allowed to grow up in this ancient Museum and among the old books, who developed a morbid curiosity for the Past, of which the books and pictures and collections taught her something; yet not all she wished to learn. She was unconsciously aided by the old man, who had been approaching his second childhood even at the time of the Great Discovery, and whose memory now continually carried him backward to the days of his youth, without the least recollection of the great intervals between. Lastly, there had come to the town, in the pursuit of his business, a sailor, restless and discontented, as is the case with all his class, questioning and independent; impatient of authority, and curiously unable to forget the old times. The sailor and the girl, between them, at first instigated and pushed on the whole business; they were joined, no doubt, by many others; but these two were the first leaders. The Chief Culprit of all, the nominal Leader— but you shall presently hear what kind of excuse could be made for him by himself. As for those whom they dragged reluctantly out of the tranquillity of oblivion, they were at first wholly drawn from the class which, at the outset, gave us so much trouble—the so-called gentle class—who desired nothing so much as to continue to live under the old conditions—namely, by the labor of others. It wanted, for these people, only the revival of memory to produce the revival of discontent. When their minds were once more filled with the thought of the things they had lost—the leadership, the land, the wealth, and with the memory of the arts which they had formerly loved—music, painting, letters—and with the actual sight, once more restored to them, of their old amusements—their dancing, their society, their singing, their games; and when the foolish old idol, Love, was once more trotted out, like an old-fashioned Guy Fawkes, decked in his silly old rainbow tints; when, night after night, they actually began to play, act, and to pretend these things, what could possibly follow but revolt, with subsequent punishment and expulsion? You shall hear. Of course, they would have been punished with expulsion had not—but everything in its place.

Five or six weeks after the first evening, which I have described at full length, the Museum was again occupied by the same company, increased by a good many more. The women came in more readily, being sooner caught with the bait of fine dress, which had such an attraction for them that the mere sight of it caused them to forget everything that had been done for them—their present tranquillity, their freedom from agitation and anxiety—and carried them back to the old time, when they wore, indeed, those dainty dresses. What they endured, besides, they do not so readily remember; but the dresses carried back their minds to the society which once filled up the whole worthless lives of these poor creatures. I say, therefore, that it was easier to attract the women than the men; for the latter, no bait at all corresponding in power could be discovered. The company assembled were engaged in much the same sort of make-believe and play-acting as on the first evening. They were dressed in the old fashion; they danced, they sang, they talked and laughed—actually they talked and laughed—though what there is, from any view of life to laugh about, I never could understand. Laughing, however, belonged to the old manners; and they had now completely recovered the old manners—anything, however foolish, which belonged to that time would have been welcomed by them. So they laughed; for the same reason, they were full of animation; and the old, old unhappy emotion which I had thought blotted out forever—restlessness—had either broken out among them or was well simulated. They were all young, save for the old man who sat in his chair coughing, and sometimes talking. Christine had dressed him in a velvet coat, which gave him great dignity, and made him look as if he was taking part in the play. I say not that the acting was not very good—of the kind. Acting of any kind could never have served any useful purpose, even in the Past. Perhaps a company of beautiful women, beautifully dressed, and of gallant men—I talk their own foolish language—amusing themselves in this way, may have given pleasure to some, but not to those among whom I was born. In the days when these things were done every night at one part of the town, in another part the men were drinking, if they had any money, and the women and children were starving. And much they concerned themselves about dancing and laughing! Laughing, indeed! My part of the town was where they starved. There was mighty little laughing among us, I can promise you.

In their masquerading they had naturally, as if it was a part of the life they represented, assumed, as I have said, the old expression of eagerness, as if there was always something wanting. And yet, I say, they laughed with each other. In the unreasonable, illogical way of the Past, although everybody always wanted everything for himself, and tried to overreach his neighbor, it was the custom to pretend that nobody wanted anything, but that everybody trusted his friend, and that everybody lived for the sole purpose of helping other people. Therefore, they shook hands continually, and grinned at each other when they met, as if they were pleased to meet and—. Well, the hypocrisies of the Past were as ridiculous as its selfishness was base.

But three of the party sat apart in the Picture Gallery. They were Christine and the two cousins, Mildred and Jack Carera. They were talking seriously and gravely.

"It comes, then," said Jack, "to this: that to all of us the Present has grown to be utterly hateful, and to one or two of us intolerable."

"Intolerable!" the other two repeated.

"We are resolved, for our own selves at least, that we will have no more of it, if we can help it. Are we not? But, Cousin Mildred, let us remember that we are only three. Perhaps, among our friends in the Museum, there may be half a dozen more who have learned to feel as strongly as ourselves. Is half a dozen a Party large enough to effect a Revolution? Remember, it is useless to think of remonstrance or petition with the College. No King, Council, or Parliament in the Past was ever half so autocratic as the College of Physicians.

"I used to read," he went on, "ages ago, about the Domination of Priests. I don't think any Rule of Priests was ever half so intolerant or so thorough as the Rule of the Physicians. They have not only deprived us of the Right of Thought, but also of the Power of Thought. The poor people cannot think. It is a truly desperate state of things. A few years more and we, too, shall sink into the same awful slough—"

"Some of us were in it already, but Christine pulled us out," said Mildred.

"Shall we ever get another chance of getting out?" Jack asked. "I think not."

"Well, Jack, go on."

"As for these evening meetings of ours, you may be very sure that they will be found out before long, and that they will be stopped. Do you think that Grout—Grout!—will suffer his beloved invention of the common dress to be trampled on? Do you imagine that Grout will suffer the revival of the old forms of society?"

"Oh," Christine replied, "if we could convert Dr. Grout!"

"Another danger," said Jack, "is, that we may all get tired of these meetings. You see, they are not the real thing. Formerly, the evening followed the day; it was the feast after the fight. Where is now the fight? And all the dancing, courting, pretty speeches, and tender looks, meant only the fore-words of Love in earnest. Now, are we ready again for Love in earnest? Can the men once more worship the women upon whom they have gazed so long unmoved? If so, we must brave the College and face the consequences. I know of two people only who are at present so much in earnest as to brave the College. They are Christine and myself."

He took the girl's hand and kissed it.

"You may add one more, Jack," said Mildred. "If you go away with Christine, take me with you; for the Present is more intolerable than any possible Future."

"That makes three, then. There may be more. Geoffrey and Dorothy are never tired of whispering and billing. Perhaps they, too, are strong enough to throw off the old terrors and to join us. But we shall see."

"I think," said Mildred, "it might depend partly on how the case is put before them. If you made them see very clearly the miseries of their present life, and made them yearn ardently for the things which they have only just remembered, some of them might follow, at all costs. But for most the College and what it holds would prove too much."

"Yet you yourself—and Christine—"

"As for me, it seems as if I remember more than anybody because I think of the sorrows of the Past. I cannot tell now how I ever came to forget those sorrows. And they are now grown so dear to me, that for the very fear of losing them again, I would give up the Gift of the College and go with you. As for Christine, she has never known at all the dread which they now pretend used to fill all our minds and poisoned all our lives. How, then, should she hesitate? Besides, she loves you, Jack—and that is enough."

"Quite enough," said Christine, smiling.

"If you remember everything," Jack went on, gravely, "you remember, Mildred, that there was something in life besides play and society. In a corner of your father's park, for instance, there was an old gray building, with a small tower and a peal of bells. The place stood in a square enclosure, in which were an old broken cross, an ancient yew-tree, two or three head-stones, and the graves of buried villagers. You

WALTER BESANT

remember that place, Mildred? You and I have often played in that ground; on weekdays we have prowled about the old building and read the monuments on the walls; on Sundays we used to sit there with all the people. Do you remember?"

Mildred clasped her hands.

"How could I ever forget?" she cried. "How could any of us forget?"

"Because Grout robbed you of your memory, my cousin. He could not rob mine."

"Alas!" she lamented, "how can we ever get that back again?"

"By memory, Mildred. It will come back presently. Think of that, and you will be less afraid to come with us. If that was able to comfort the world formerly when the world was full of life and joy and needed so little comfort, what should it not do for you now, when the world is so dull and dismal, and the Awful Present is so long that it seems never to have had a beginning, just as it promises never to have an end. Courage, Cousin Mildred.

"And now," he went on, after a pause, "for my plan. My ship is bound for any port to which the College may despatch her. She must sail in about four or five weeks. I shall take you both on board. Christine will be my wife—you shall be our companion. Perhaps one or two more may go with us. We shall take certain things that we shall want. I can procure all these without the least suspicion, and we shall sail to an island of which I know, where the air is always warm and the soil is fruitful. There the sailors shall land us and shall sail away, unless they please to join us. And there we will live out our allotted lives, without asking anything of the College. The revival of that lost part of your memory, Mildred, will serve you in place of what they could have given you. You agree? Well, that is settled, then. Let us go back."

But, as you shall see, this plan was never carried out.

When all went away that evening, Mildred remained behind.

"Christine," she said, "I have something to tell you. Take me somewhere—to some dark place—where we can whisper."

One might as well have talked at the top of his voice, just where they were, for any chance of being heard; but guilt made the woman tremble.

"Come into the Picture Gallery," said Christine, leading the way. "No one can hear what we say there. My dear, in the old days when people were going to conspire they always began by going to dark galleries, vaults, and secret places. This is quite delightful. I feel like a conspirator."

"Don't laugh at me, dear," said Mildred; "for, indeed, when you have heard what I have to say, you will feel very much more like a conspirator."

The room was in darkness, but for the moonlight which poured in through the windows of one side, and made queer work with the pictures on which it fell. At the end the moonlight shone through the door, hardly ever used, which led from the Gallery into the Garden of the College beyond.

"What is that?" Mildred caught Christine by the hand.

"It is the door leading into the College Gardens. How came it open?"

"Have you a key?"

"I suppose there is a key on the old rusty bunch hanging up in the Museum, but I do not know—I have never tried the keys. Who could have opened it?"

Christine walked down the Gallery hastily, Mildred following. The door was standing wide open.

"Who has done this?" asked Christine, again. "I cannot tell who could have opened the door, or why. It has never been opened before."

Mildred shuddered. "It is thrown open for some mischief," she said; "we shall find out soon enough by whom."

Then they looked out through the door into the Garden of the College. The door faced a semicircular lawn run wild with rank grass never shorn; behind the lawn were trees; and the moonlight lay on all.

Suddenly the girls caught hands and shrank back into the door-way, for a tall form emerged from the trees and appeared upon the lawn, where he walked with hanging head and hands clasped behind his back.

"It is the Arch Physician!" Christine whispered.

"It is Harry Linister," Mildred murmured.

Then they retreated within and shut the door noiselessly; but they could not lock or fasten it.

"I can see that part of the Garden from a window in the Library," said Christine. "He walks there every morning and every evening. He is always alone. He always hangs his head, and he always looks fit to cry for trouble. What is the good of being Arch Physician, if you cannot have things done as you want?"

"My dear," said Mildred, "I am afraid you do not quite understand. In the old days—I mean not quite the dear old days, but in the time when people still discussed things and we had not been robbed of memory and of understanding—it was very well known that the Arch Physician was out-voted in the College by Grout and his Party."

"By Doctor Grout?"

"My dear, Grout was never a Doctor. He only calls himself Doctor. I remember when Grout was an ignorant man taken into Professor Linister's Laboratory to wash up the pots and bottles. He was thin, just as he is now—a short, dark, and sour-faced man, with bright eyes. Oh, a clever man, I dare say, but ignorant, and full of hatred for the class of culture and refinement. It was Grout who led the Party which took away land and wealth from individuals and transferred all to the State. It was Grout who ordered the Massacre of the Old. It was Grout who invented the horrible cruelty of the Common Dress. It was Grout who made the College what it is—not what it was meant to be. It was originally the Guardian of Life and Health. It has become the Tyrant of the People. It has destroyed everything—everything that makes life possible—and it tells the People to be happy because they live. It is Grout—Grout!—who has done this. Not the Arch Physician. Not Harry Linister."

"Why do you say 'Harry Linister,' Mildred?"

"My dear, I think that of all women living I have the greatest cause to hate the Great Discovery, because it robbed me of my lover."

"Tell me how, dear."

"I told you, Christine, that the revival of the Past was the revival of sorrows that I would never again forget. Listen, then, and I will tell you what they were. When the Great Discovery was announced, Harry Linister was already a man well known in Science, Christine; but he was also well known in Society as well. Science did not prevent him from falling in love. And he fell in love with—me. Yes—with me. We met that fatal evening at the Royal Institution, and we arranged, before the Lecture, where we should meet after the Lecture. My dear, I knew very well what he was going to say; and—oh, my poor heart!—how happy I was to think of it! There was nobody in London more clever, more handsome, and more promising than Harry. He was rich, if that mattered anything to me; he was already a Fellow of the Royal Society, for some great discoveries he had made; everybody said that a splendid career was before him—and he loved me, Christine."

"Well?"

"Well, the news of the Great Discovery carried him out of himself. He forgot his love—and me—and everything. When his eyes fell upon me again, I know not how long after, I was in the hideous Common Dress, and he no more recognized me than a stranger would recognize one out of a herd of sheep."

"How could he forget? Do you think that Jack could ever forget me?"

"I am sure he will not, at any rate. Now, Christine, I am going to try something serious. I am going to try to convert the Arch Physician himself!"

"Mildred!"

"Why not? He is still a man, I suppose. Nobody ever thought that Grout was a man; but Harry Linister was once a man, and should be still. And if he have a memory as well as eyes, why—then—" she sighed. "But that would be too much, indeed, to hope."

"What if you win him, Mildred?"

"Why, child, he used to love me. Is not that enough? Besides, he *knows the Great Secret*. If we have him with us, we have also with us all the people whom we can shake, push, or prick out of their present miserable apathy. Why did we ever agree to the stupid work day by day? We began by fighting for the wealth, and those who survived enjoyed it. Why did we not go on fighting? Why did we consent to wear this hideous dress? Why did we consent to be robbed of our intelligence, and to be reduced to the condition of sheep? All because the College had the Great Secret, and they made the People think that to forego that one advantage was worse than all other evils that could happen to them. It was Grout—the villany of Grout—that did it. Now, if we can by any persuasion draw the Arch Physician over to ourselves, we win the cause for all those who join us, because they will lose nothing."

"How will you win him, Mildred?"

"Child, you are young; you do not know the history of Delilah, of the Sirens, of Circe, of Cleopatra, of Vivien, of a thousand Fair Ladies who have witched away the senses of great men, so that they have become as wax in the hands of their conquerors. Poor Harry! His heart was not always as hard as stone, nor was it always as heavy as lead. I would witch him, if I could, for his own happiness, poor lad!—and for mine as well. Let him only come with us, bringing the precious Secret, and we are safe!"

IT HAS BEEN OBSERVED THAT many hard things were said concerning me—Grout—and that I have, nevertheless, written them down. First the things are all true, and I rejoice to think of the part that I have always played in the conduct of the People since the Great Discovery enabled me to obtain a share in that conduct. Next, it may be asked how I became possessed of this information. That you shall presently understand.

All that I have done in my public capacity—as for private life, I never had any, except that one goes into a private room for sleep—has been for the Advancement of Humanity. In order to effect this advance with the greater ease, I found it necessary to get rid of useless hands—therefore the Old were sacrificed; to adopt one common standard in everything, so that there should be the same hours of work for all, the same food both in quantity and quality, the same dress, and the same housing. As by far the greater number belong to what were formerly known as the lower classes, everything has been a gain for them. Now, a gain for the majority is a gain for Humanity. As for the abolition of disturbing emotions, such as Love, Jealousy, Ambition, Study, Learning, and the like, the loss of them is, of course, pure gain. In short, I willingly set down all that may be or has been said against myself, being quite satisfied to let the truth speak for itself. I have now to tell of the Daring Attempt made upon the Fidelity of the Chief—the Arch Physician himself.

VI

The Arch Physician

The Arch Physician generally walked in the College Gardens for an hour or so every forenoon. They are very large and spacious Gardens, including plantations of trees, orchards, ferneries, lawns, flower-beds, and shrubberies. In one corner is a certain portion which, having been left entirely alone by the gardeners, has long since become like a tangled coppice, rather than a garden, covered with oaks and elms and all kinds of trees, and overgrown with thick underwoods. It was in this wild and secluded part that Dr. Linister daily walked. It lay conveniently at the back of his own residence, and adjoining the Museum and Picture Gallery. No one came here except himself, and but for the beaten path which his footsteps had made in their daily walk, the place would have become entirely overgrown. As it was, there were thick growths of holly and of yew; tall hawthorn-trees, wild roses spreading about among brambles; ferns grew tall in the shade, and under the great trees there was a deep shadow even on the brightest day. In this neglected wood there were creatures of all kinds—rabbits, squirrels, snakes, moles, badgers, weasels, and stoats. There were also birds of all kinds in the wood, and in the stream that ran through the place there were otters. In this solitary place Dr. Linister walked every day and meditated. The wildness and the solitude pleased and soothed him. I have already explained that he had always, from the outset, been most strongly opposed to the policy of the majority, and that he was never free from a certain melancholy. Perhaps he meditated on the world as he would have made it, had he been able to have his own way.

I HAVE HEARD THAT MUCH was said among the Rebels about my conduct during these events, as wanting in Gratitude. In the first place, if it is at all necessary for me to defend my conduct, let me point out that my duty to the Authority of the House must come before everything—certainly before the claims of private gratitude. In the second place, I owe no gratitude at all to Dr. Linister, or to anybody. I have made myself. Whatever I have done, alone I have done it, and unaided. Dr. Linister, it is very true, received me into his laboratory

WALTER BESANT

as bottle-washer and servant. Very good. He paid me my wages, and I did his work for him. Much room for gratitude there. He looked for the proper discharge of the work, and I looked for the regular payment of the wages. Where does the gratitude come in? He next taught me the elements of science. To be sure, he wanted the simpler part of his experiments conducted by a skilled, not an ignorant, hand. Therefore he taught me those elements. The better skilled the hand, the more he could depend upon the successful conduct of his research. Therefore, when he found that he could depend upon my eye and hand, he taught me more, and encouraged me to work on my own account, and gave me the best books to read. Very good. All for his own purposes.

What happened next? Presently, Grout the Bottle-washer became so important in the laboratory that he became Grout the Assistant, or Demonstrator; and another Bottle-washer was appointed—a worthy creature who still performs that useful Function, and desires nothing more than to wash the bottles truly and thoroughly. Next, Grout became known outside the laboratory; many interesting and important discoveries were made by Grout; then Grout became too big a man to be any longer Dr. Linister's Assistant; he had his own laboratory; Grout entered upon his own field of research. This was a practical field, and one in which he quickly surpassed all others.

Remember that Dr. Linister never claimed, or looked for, gratitude. He was much too wise a man. On all occasions, when it was becoming in him, he spoke in the highest terms of his former Assistant's scientific achievements.

There was, in fact, no question of Gratitude at all.

As for personal friendship, the association of years, the bond of union, or work in common—these are mere phrases, the worn-out old phrases of the vanished Past. Besides, there never was any personal friendship. Quite the contrary. Dr. Linister was never able to forget that in the old time I had been the servant and he the master. Where equality has been so long established, the continual reminder of former inequality is galling.

Dr. Linister, indeed, was always antipathetic from the beginning. Except over a research, we could have nothing in common. In the old days he was what they called a gentleman; he was also a scholar; he used to play music and write verses; he would act and dance and sing, and do all kinds of things; he was one of those men who always wanted to do everything that other men can do, and to do it as well as other men could do it. So that, though he was a great scientific worker, he spent half his day at his club, or at his sports, or in Society; that is to say, with the women—and mostly, I think, among the games and amusements of the women. There was every day, I remember, a great running to and fro of page-boys with notes from them; and he was always ready to leave any, even the most important work, just to run after a woman's caprice.

As for me, I never had any school education at all; I never had anything to do with Society; the sight of a woman always filled me with contempt for the man who could waste time in running after a creature who knew no science, never cared for any, and was so wont to disfigure her natural figure by the way she crowded on her misshapen clothes that no one could guess what it was like beneath them. As for music, art, and the rest of it, I never asked so much as what they meant; after I began to make my way, I had the laboratory for work, play, and all.

When, again, it came to the time when the Property question became acute, and we attempted to solve it by a Civil War, although Dr. Linister adhered to his determination not to leave his laboratory, his sympathies were always with individualism. Nay, he never disguised his opinion, but was accustomed regularly to set it forth at our Council meetings in the House of Life—that the abolition of property and the establishment of the perfect Socialism were the greatest blows ever inflicted upon civilization. It is not, however, civilization which the College advances, but Science—which is a very different thing—and the Scientific End of Humanity. The gradual extinction of all the emotions—love, jealousy, ambition, rivalry—Dr. Linister maintained, made life so poor a thing that painless extinction would be the very best thing possible for the whole race. It is useless to point out, to one so prejudiced, the enormous advantage gained in securing constant tranquillity of mind. He was even, sometimes, an advocate for the revival of fighting—fighting, the old barbarous way of settling disputes, in which lives were thrown away by thousands on a single field. Nor would he ever agree with the majority of the House that the only End of Humanity is mere existence, at which Science should always aim, prolonged without exertion, thought, care, or emotion of any kind.

In fact, according to the contention of my followers and myself, the Triumph of Science is as follows: The Philosopher finds a creature, extremely short-lived at the best, liable to every kind of disease and suffering from external causes, torn to pieces from within by all kinds of conflicting emotions; a creature most eager and insatiate of appetite, fiery and impetuous, quarrelsome and murderous, most difficult to drive or lead, guided only by its own selfish desires, tormented by intellectual doubts and questions which can never be answered. The Philosopher works upon this creature until he has moulded it into another so different that no one would perceive any likeness to the original creature. The new creature is immortal; it is free from disease or the possibility of disease; it has no emotions, no desires, and no intellectual restlessness. It breathes, eats, sleeps.

Such is my idea of Science Triumphant. It was never Dr. Linister's.

In manners, the Arch Physician preserved the old manners of courtesy and deference which were the fashion when he was brought up. His special work had been for many years the study of the so-called incurable diseases, such as asthma, gout, rheumatism, and so forth. For my own part, my mind, since I became Suffragan, has always been occupied with Administration, having steadily in view the Triumph of Science. I have, with this intention, made the Social Equality real and complete from every point; I have also endeavored to simplify labor, to enlarge the production and the distribution of food by mechanical means, and thus to decrease the necessity for thought, contrivance, and the exercise of ingenuity. Most of our work is so subdivided that no one understands more than the little part of it which occupies him for four hours every day. Workmen who know the whole process are impossible. They ask, they inquire, they want to improve; when their daily task is but a bit of mechanical drudgery, they do it without thought and they come away. Since labor is necessary, let it be as mechanical as possible, so that the head may not be in the least concerned with the work of the hand. In this—my view of things—the Arch Physician could never be brought to acquiesce. Had he been able to have his own way, the whole of my magnificent scheme would have been long ago destroyed and rendered impossible. I suppose it was this impossibility of having his own way which afflicted him with so profound a melancholy. His face was always sad, because he could never reconcile himself to the doctrine of human equality, without which the Perfection of Man is impossible.

It will be seen, in short, that the Arch Physician and myself held hardly a single view in common. But he had been elected to his post, and I to mine. We shared between us the Great Secret; and if my views prevailed in our Council, it was due either to my own power of impressing my views upon my colleagues, or to the truth and justice of those views.

But as to gratitude, there was no room or cause for any.

As, then, Dr. Linister walked to and fro upon the open space outside the Picture Gallery, his hands behind him, his head hanging, and his thoughts I know not where, he became conscious of something that was out of the usual order. When one lives as we live, one day following another, each like the one which went before, little departures from the accustomed order disturb the mind. For many, many years the Doctor had not given a thought to the Picture Gallery or to the door. Yet, because it stood open, and he had been accustomed to see it closed, he was disturbed, and presently lifted his head and discovered the cause.

The door stood open. Why? What was the door? Then he remembered what it was, and whither it led. It opened into the ancient Picture Gallery, the very existence of which he had forgotten, though every day he saw the door and the building itself. The Picture Gallery! It was full of the pictures painted in the last few years before the Great Discovery; that is to say, it was full of the life which he had long ago lived—nay, he lived it still. As he stood hesitating without the door, that life came back to him with a strange yearning and sinking of the heart. He had never, you see, ceased to regret it, nor had he ever forgotten it. And now he was tempted to look upon it again. As well might a monk in the old times look upon a picture of fair women years after he had forsworn love.

He hesitated, his knees trembling, for merely thinking what was within. Then he yielded to the temptation, and went into the Gallery.

The morning sun streamed through the window and lay upon the floor; the motes danced in the sunshine; the Gallery was quite empty; but on the walls hung, one above the other, five or six in each row, the pictures of the Past. In some the pigments were faded; crimson was pale-pink; green was gray; red was brown; but the figures were there, and the Life which he had lost once more flashed upon his brain. He saw the women whom once he had loved so much; they were lying on soft couches, gazing upon him with eyes which made his heart to beat and his whole frame to tremble; they were dancing; they were in boats, dressed in dainty summer costume; they were playing lawn-tennis; they were in drawing-rooms, on horseback, on lawns, in gardens; they were being wooed by their lovers. What more? They were painted in fancy costumes, ancient costumes, and even with no costume at all. And the more he looked, the more his cheek glowed and his heart beat. Where had they gone—the women of his youth?

Suddenly he heard the tinkling of a musical instrument. It was a thing they used to call a zither. He started, as one awakened out of a dream. Then he heard a voice singing; and it sang the same song he had heard that night five or six weeks ago—his own song:

> *"The girls they laugh, the girls they cry,*
> *'What shall their guerdon be?—*
> *Alas! that some must fall and die!—*
> *Bring forth our gauds to see.*
> *'Twere all too slight, give what we might.'*
> *Up spoke a soldier tall:*
> *'Oh! Love is worth the whole broad earth;*
> *Oh! Love is worth the whole broad earth;*
> *Give that, you give us all!'"*

This time, however, it was another voice—a fuller and richer voice—which sang those words.

Dr. Linister started again when the voice began. He changed color, and his cheek grew pale.

"Heavens!" he murmured. "Are there phantoms in the air? What does it mean? This is the second time—my own song—the foolish old song—my own air—the foolish, tinkling air that they used to like! And the voice—I remember the voice—whose voice is it? I remember the voice—whose voice is it?"

He looked round him again, at the pictures, as if to find among them the face he sought. The pictures showed all the life of the Past; the ball-room with the dancers; the sports of the field; the drive in the afternoon, the ride in the morning; the bevy of girls; the soldiers and the sailors; the streets crowded with people; the vile slums and the picturesque blackguardism of the City—but not the face he wanted. Then he left off looking for the singer, and began to think of the faces before him.

"On every face," he said, "there is unsatisfied desire. Yet they are the happier for that very dissatisfaction. Yes—they are the happier." He paused before a painted group of street children; some were playing over the gutter; some were sitting on door-steps, carrying babies as big as themselves; one was sucking a piece of orange-peel picked up on the pavement; one was gnawing a crust. They were all ragged and half starved. "Yet," said the Arch Physician, "they are happy. But we have no children now. In those days they could paint and draw—and we have lost the Art. Great heavens!" he cried, impatiently, "we have lost every

Art. Cruel! cruel!" Then from within there broke upon his ears a strain of music. It was so long since he had heard any music that at first it took away his breath. Wonderful that a mere sound such as that of music should produce such an effect upon a man of science! "Oh," he sighed, heavily, "we have even thrown away that! Yet—where—where does the music come from? Who plays it?"

While he listened, carried away by the pictures and by the music and by his own thoughts to the Past, his mind full of the Past, it did not surprise him in the least that there came out from the door between the Gallery and the Museum a young lady belonging absolutely to the Past. There was no touch of the Present about her at all. She did not wear the regulation dress; she did not wear the flat cap.

"It is," said Dr. Linister, "the Face that belongs to the Voice. I know it now. Where did I see it last? To whom does it belong?"

She stood for a few moments in the sunshine. Behind her was a great picture all crimson and purple, a mass of flaming color, before which her tall and slight figure, dressed in a delicate stuff of soft creamy color, stood clearly outlined. The front of the dress—at least that part which covered the throat to the waist—was of some warmer color; there were flowers at her left shoulder; her hair was braided tightly round her head; round her neck was a ribbon with something hanging from it; she wore brown gloves, and carried a straw hat dangling in her hand. It was, perhaps, the sunshine which made her eyes so bright, her cheek so glowing, her rosy lips so quivering.

She stood there, looking straight down the Hall, as if she saw no one.

Dr. Linister gazed and turned pale; his cheeks were so white that you might have thought him about to faint; he reeled and trembled.

"Good God!" he murmured, falling back upon the interjection of the Past, "we have lost the Beauty of women! Oh, Fools! Fools! We have thrown all away—all—and for what?"

Then the girl came swiftly down the Hall towards him. A smile of welcome was on her lips; a blush upon her cheek; her eyes looked up and dropped again, and again looked up and once more dropped.

Then she stopped before him and held out both her hands.

"Harry Linister!" she cried, as if surprised, and with a little laugh, "how long is it since last we met?"

VII

THE FIDELITY OF JOHN LAX

That morning, while I was in my private laboratory, idly turning over certain Notes on experiments conducted for the artificial manufacture of food, I was interrupted by a knock at the door.

My visitor was the Porter of the House of Life, our most trusted servant, John Lax. His duty it was to sleep in the House—his chamber being that ancient room over the South Porch—to inspect the furnaces and laboratories after the work of the day was closed, and at all times to keep an eye upon the Fabric itself, so that it should in no way fall out of repair. His orders were also to kill any strangers who might try to force their way into the House on any pretence whatever.

He was a stout, sturdy fellow, vigorous and strong, though the Great Discovery had found him nearly forty years of age; his hair, though it had gone bald on the top, was still thick on the sides, and gave him a terrifying appearance under his cap of scarlet and gold. He carried a great halberd as a wand of office, and his coat and cap matched each other for color and for gold embroidery. Save as representing the authority of the House and College, I would never have allowed such a splendid appearance to any one.

"What have you come to tell me, John?" I asked.

I may explain that I had always found John Lax useful in keeping me informed as to the internal condition of the College and its Assistants—what was said and debated—what opinions were advanced, by what men, and so forth.

"In the College itself, Suffragan," he said, "and in the House, things are mighty dull and quiet. Blessed if a little Discontent or a Mutiny, or something, wouldn't be worth having, just to shake up the lot. There's not even a grumbler left. A little rising and a few heads broken, and we should settle down again, quiet and contented again."

"Don't talk like a fool, John."

"Well, Suffragan, you like to hear all that goes on. I wonder what you'll say to what I'm going to tell you now?"

"Go on, John. What is it?"

"It's irregular, Suffragan, but your Honor is above the Law; and, before beginning a long story—mind you, a most important story it is—"

"What is it about? Who's in it?"

"Lots of the People are in it. They don't count. He's in it now—come!"

"He?"

John Lax had pointed over his shoulder so clearly in the direction of the Arch Physician's residence that I could not but understand. Yet I pretended.

"He, John? Who is he?"

"The Arch Physician is in it. There! Now, Suffragan, bring out that bottle and a glass, and I can then tell you the story, without fear of ill consequences to my throat that was once delicate."

I gave him the bottle and a glass, and, after drinking a tumblerful of whiskey (forbidden to the People) he began.

Certain reasons, he said, had made him suspicious as to what went on at night in the Museum during the last few weeks. The lights were up until late at night. Once he tried the doors, and found that they were locked. He heard the playing of music within, and the sound of many voices.

Now, there is, as I told John Lax at this point, no law against the assemblage of the People, nor against their sitting up, or singing and playing together. I had, to be sure, hoped that they had long ceased to desire to meet together, and had quite forgotten how to make music.

He remembered, John Lax went on to say, that there was a door leading into the Picture Gallery from the College Garden—a door of which he held the key.

He opened this door quietly, and then, night after night, he crept into the Picture Gallery, and watched what went on through the door, which opened upon the Museum. He had found, in fact, a place close by the door, where, hidden behind a group of statuary, he could watch and listen in almost perfect security.

I then heard, to my amazement, how a small company of the People were every night carrying on a revival of the Past; not with the laudable intention of disgusting themselves with the horrors of that time, but exactly the contrary. It was only the pleasant side of that time—the evening life of the rich and careless—which these foolish persons reproduced.

They had, in fact, gone so far, John Lax told me, as to fall in love with that time, to deride the Present, and to pour abuse upon my name—mine—as the supposed chief author of the Social Equality. This was very well for a beginning. This was a startling awakener out of a Fool's Paradise. True, the company was small; they might be easily dispersed or isolated; means might be found to terrify them into submission. Yet it gave me a rude shock.

"I've had my suspicions," John Lax continued, "ever since one morning when I looked into the Museum and see that young gal dressed up and carrying on before the looking-glass, more like—well, more like an actress at the Pav, as they used to make 'em, than like a decent woman. But now there's more." He stopped and whispered, hoarsely, "Suffragan, I've just come from a little turn about the Garden. Outside the Picture Gallery, where there's a bit o' turf and a lot of trees all standin' around, there's a very curious sight to see this minute; and if you'll get up and go along o' me, Suffragan, you'll be pleased—you will, indeed—astonished and pleased you will be."

I obeyed. I arose and followed this zealous servant. He led me to a part of the Garden which I did not know; it was the place of which I have spoken. Here, amid a great thick growth of underwood, he took me into the ruins of an old garden or tool-house, built of wood, but the planks were decaying and were starting apart.

"Stand there, and look and listen," whispered John Lax, grinning.

The open planks commanded a view of a semicircular lawn, where the neglected grass had grown thick and rank. Almost under my eyes there was sitting upon a fallen trunk a woman, fantastically dressed—against the Rules—and at her feet lay none other than the Arch Physician himself! Then, indeed, I pricked up my ears and listened with all my might.

"Are we dreaming, Mildred?" he murmured. "Are we dreaming?"

"No, Harry; we have all been dreaming for a long, long time—never mind how long. Just now we are not dreaming, we are truly awake. You are my old playfellow, and I am your old sweetheart," she said, with a little blush. "Tell me what you are doing—always in your laboratory. I suppose, always finding some new secrets. Does it make you any happier, Harry, to be always finding something new?"

"It is the only thing that makes life endurable—to discover the secrets of Nature. For what other purpose do we live?"

"Then, Harry, for what purpose do the rest of us live, who do not investigate those secrets? Can women be happy in no other way? We do not prosecute any kind of research, you know."

"Happy? Are we in the Present or the Past, Mildred?"

He looked about him, as if expecting to see the figures of the Pictures in the Gallery walking about upon the grass.

"Just now, Harry, we are in the Past. We are back—we two together—in the glorious and beautiful Past, where everything was delightful. Outside this place there is the horrible Present. You have made the Present for us, and therefore you ought to know what it is. Let me look at you, Harry. Why, the old look is coming back to your eyes. Take off that black gown, Harry, and throw it away, while you are with me. So. You are now my old friend again, and we can talk. You are no longer the President of the Holy College, the terrible and venerable Arch Physician, the Guardian of the House of Life. You are plain Harry Linister again. Tell me, then, Harry, are you happy in this beautiful Present that you have made?"

"No, Mildred; I am never happy."

"Then why not unmake the Present? Why not return to the Past?"

"It is impossible. We might go back to the Past for a little; but it would become intolerable again, as it did before. Formerly there was no time for any of the fleeting things of life to lose their rapture. All things were enjoyed for a moment, and then vanished. Now"—he sighed wearily—"they last—they last. So that there is nothing left for us but the finding of new secrets. And for you, Mildred?"

"I have been in a dream," she replied. "Oh, a long, long nightmare, that has never left me, day or night. I don't know how long it has lasted. But it has lifted at last, thank GOD!"

The Arch Physician started and looked astonished.

"It seems a long time," he said, "since I heard those words. I thought we had forgotten—"

"It was a dream of no change, day after day. Nothing happened. In the morning we worked; in the afternoon we rested; in the evening we took food; at night we slept. And the mind was dead. There were no books to read; there was nothing to talk about; there was nothing to hope. Always the same work—a piece of work that nobody cared to do—a mechanical piece of work. Always the same dress—the same hideous, horrible dress. We were all alike; there was nothing at all to distinguish us. The Past seemed forgotten."

"Nothing can be ever forgotten," said Dr. Linister; "but it may be put away for a time."

"Oh, when I think of all that we had forgotten, it seems terrible! Yet we lived—how could we live?—it was not life. No thought, no care, about anything. Every one centred in himself, careless of his neighbor. Why, I did not know so much as the occupants of the rooms next to my own. Men looked on women, and women on men, without thought or emotion. Love was dead—Life was Death? Harry, it was a most dreadful dream. And in the night there used to come a terrible nightmare of nothingness! It was as if I floated alone in ether, far from the world or life, and could find nothing—nothing—for the mind to grasp or think of. And I woke at the point of madness. A dreadful dream! And yet we lived. Rather than go back to that most terrible dream, I would—I would—"

She clasped her forehead with her hand and looked about her with haggard eyes.

"Yes, yes," said Dr. Linister; "I ought to have guessed your sufferings—by my own. Yet I have had my laboratory."

"Then I was shaken out of the dream by a girl—by Christine. And now we are resolved—some of us—at all costs and hazards—yes, even if we are debarred from the Great Discovery—to—live—again—to live—again!" she repeated, slowly. "Do you know, Harry, what that means? To go back—to live again! Only think what that means."

He was silent.

"Have you forgotten, Harry," she asked, softly, "what that means?"

"No," he said. "I remember everything; but I am trying to understand. The accursed Present is around and above me, like a horrible black Fog. How can we lift it? How can we live again?"

"Some of us have found out a way. In the morning we put on the odious uniform, and do our allotted task among the poor wretches who are still in that bad dream of never-ending monotony. We sit among them, silent ourselves, trying to disguise the new light that has come back to our eyes, in the Public Hall. In the evening we come here, put on the old dresses, and live the old life."

"It is wonderful," he said. "I knew all along that human nature would one day assert itself again. I told Grout so. He has always been quite wrong!"

"Grout! What does Grout know of civilized life? Grout! Why, he was your own bottle-washer—a common servant. He thought it was justice to reduce everybody to his own level, and happiness for them to remain there! Grout! Why, he has only one idea—to make us mere machines. Oh, Harry!" she said, reproach in her eyes, "you are Arch Physician, and you cannot alter things!"

"No; I have the majority of the College against me."

"Am I looking well, Harry, after all these years?"

She suddenly changed her voice and manner and laughed, and turned her face to meet his. Witch! Abominable Witch!

"Well, Mildred, was it yesterday that I loved you? Was the Great Discovery made only yesterday? Oh, you look lovelier than ever!"

"Lovely means worthy of love, Harry. But you have killed love."

"No, no. Love died. We did not kill love. Why did the men cease to love the women? Was it that they saw them every day, and so grew tired of them?"

"Perhaps it was because you took from us the things that might have kept love alive; music, art, literature, grace, culture, society—everything."

"We did not take them. They died."

"And then you dressed us all alike, in the most hideous costume ever invented."

"It was Grout's dress."

"What is the good of being Arch Physician if one cannot have his own way?"

Harry sighed.

"My place is in the laboratory," he said. "I experiment, and I discover. The Suffragan administers. It has always been the rule. Yet you live again, Mildred. Tell me more. I do not understand how you contrive to live again."

"We have a little company of twenty or thirty, who meet together in the evening after the dinner is over. No one else ever comes to the Museum. As soon as it is dark, you know very well, the People all creep home and go to bed; but my friends come here. It was Christine who began it. She found or made the dresses for us; she beguiled us into forgetting the Present and going back to the Past. Now we have succeeded in caring nothing at all about the Present. We began by pretending. It is no longer pretence. The Past lives again, and we hate the Present. Oh, we hate and loathe it!"

"Yes, yes. But how do you revive the Past?"

"We have dances. You used to dance very well formerly, my dear Harry. That was before you walked every day in a grand Procession, and took the highest place in the Public Hall. I wonder if you could dance again? Nature's secrets are not so heavy that they would clog your feet, are they? We sing and play: the old music has been found, and we are beginning to play it properly again. We talk; we act little drawing-room plays; sometimes we draw or paint; and—oh, Harry!—the men have begun again to make Love—real, ardent Love! All the dear old passions are reviving. We are always finding other poor creatures like ourselves, who were once ladies and gentlemen, and now are aimless and soulless; and we recruit them."

"What will Grout say when he finds it out?"

"He can never make us go back to the Present again. So far, I defy Grout, Harry."

The Arch Physician sighed.

"The old life!" he said; "the old life! I will confess, Mildred, that I have never forgotten it—not for a day; and I have never ceased to regret that it was not continued."

"Grout pulled it to pieces; but we will revive it."

"If it could be revived; but that is impossible."

"Nothing is impossible to you—nothing—to you. Consider, Harry," she whispered. "You have the Secret."

He started and changed color.

"Yes, yes," he said; "but what then?"

"Come and see the old life revived. Come this evening; come, dear Harry." She laid a hand upon his arm. "Come, for auld lang syne. Can the old emotions revive again, even in the breast of the Arch Physician?"

His eyes met hers. He trembled—a sure sign that the old spirit was reviving in him. Then he spoke in a kind of murmur:

"I have been living alone so long—so long—that I thought there was nothing left but solitude forever. Grout likes it. He will have it that loneliness belongs to the Higher Life."

"Come to us," she replied, her hand still on his arm, her eyes turned so as to look into his. Ah, shameless Witch! "We are not lonely; we talk; we exchange looks and smiles. We have begun again to practise the old arts; we have begun to read in each other's souls. Old thoughts that we had long forgotten are pouring back into our minds; it is strange to find them there again. Come, Harry; forget the laboratory for a while, and come with us; but come without Grout. The mere aspect of Grout would cause all our innocent joys to take flight and vanish. Come! Be no more the Sacred Head of the Holy College, but my dear old friend and companion, Harry Linister, who might have been but for the Great Discovery—but that is foolish. Come, Harry; come this evening."

VIII

THE ARCH TRAITOR

I dismissed John Lax, charging him with the most profound secrecy. I knew, and had known for a long time, that this man, formerly the avowed enemy of aristocrats, nourished an extraordinary hatred for the Arch Physician, and therefore I was certain that he would keep silence.

I resolved that I would myself keep a watch, and, if possible, be present at the meeting of this evening. What would happen I knew not, nor could I tell what to do; there are no laws in our community to prevent such meetings. If the Arch Physician chooses to attend such a play-acting, how is he to be prevented? But I would myself watch. You shall hear how I was rewarded.

Dr. Linister was, as usual, melancholy and preoccupied at Supper. He said nothing of what he intended. As for me, I looked about the Hall to see if there were any whom I could detect, from any unnatural restlessness, as members of this dangerous company; but I could see none, except the girl Christine, whose vivacity might be allowed on the score of youth. The face of John Lax, it is true, as he sat at the lowest place of our table, betokened an ill-suppressed joy and an eagerness quite interesting to one who understood the meaning of these emotions. Poor John Lax! Never again shall we find one like unto him for zeal and strength and courage.

I waited until half-past nine o'clock; then I sallied forth.

It was a dark night and still. There was no moon; the sky was cloudy; no wind was in the air, and from time to time there were low rumblings of distant thunder.

I made my way cautiously and noiselessly through the dark Garden to the entrance of the Picture Gallery, which the faithful John Lax had left open for me. I ventured, with every precaution, into the Gallery. It seemed quite empty, but at the end there was a door opening into the Museum, which poured a narrow stream of light straight down the middle of the Gallery. I crept along the dark wall, and presently found myself at the end close to this door. And here I came upon the group of statuary of which John Lax had told me where I could crouch and hide in perfect safety, unseen myself, yet able to see everything that went on within.

I confess that even the revelations of John Lax had not prepared me for the scene which met my eyes. There were thirty or forty men and women present; the room was lit up; there were flowers in vases set about; there was a musical instrument, at which one sat down and sang. When she had finished, everybody began to laugh and talk. Then another sat down and began to play, and then they went out upon the floor two by two, in pairs, and began to twirl round like teetotums. As for their dresses, I never saw the like; for the women were dressed in frocks of silk—white, pink, cream-colored, trimmed with lace; with jewels on their arms and necks, and long white gloves, and flowers in their hair. In their hands they carried fans, and their dresses were low, exposing their necks, and so much of their arms as was not covered up with gloves. And they looked excited and eager. The expression which I had striven so long to impart to their faces, that of tranquillity, was gone. The old unhappy eagerness, with flashing eyes, flushed cheeks, and panting breath, was come back to them again. Heavens! what could be done? As for the men, they wore a black-cloth dress—all alike—why, then, did they dislike the regulation blue flannel?—with a large white shirt-front and white ties and white gloves. And they, too, were full of the restless eagerness and excitement. So different were they all from the men and women whom I had observed day after day in the Public Hall, that I could remember not one except the girl Christine, and—and—yes, among them there was none other than the Arch Physician himself, laughing, talking, dancing among the rest.

I could see perfectly well through the open door, and I was quite certain that no one could see me; but I crouched lower behind the marble group when they began to come out two by two, and to talk together in the dark Gallery.

First came the girl Christine and the sailor, Jack Carera. Him at all events I remembered. They took each other's hands and began to kiss each other, and to talk the greatest nonsense imaginable. No one would ever believe that sane people could possibly talk such nonsense. Then they went back and another pair came out, and went on in the same ridiculous fashion. One has been to a Theatre in the old time and heard a couple of lovers talking nonsense on the stage; but never on any stage did I ever hear such false, extravagant, absurd stuff talked as I did when I lay hidden behind that group in marble.

Presently I listened with interest renewed, because the pair which came into the Gallery was none other than the pair I had that morning watched in the Garden—the Arch Physician and the woman he called Mildred, though now I should hardly have known her, because she was so dressed up and disguised. She looked, indeed, a very splendid creature; not in the least like a plain woman. And this, I take it, was what these would-be great ladies desired—not to be taken as plain women. Yet they were, in spite of their fine clothes, plain and simple women just as much as any wench of Whitechapel in the old time.

"Harry," she said, "I thank you from my very heart for coming. Now we shall have hope."

"What hope?" he replied, "what hope? What can I do for you while the majority of the College continue to side with Grout? What hope can I bring you?"

"Never mind the Majority. Consider, Harry. You have the Great Secret. Let us all go away together and found a new colony, where we will have no Grout; and we will live our own lives. Do you love me, Harry?"

"Love you, Mildred? Oh"—he sighed deeply—"it is a stream that has been dammed up all these years!"

"What keeps us here?" asked the girl. "It is that in your hands lies the Great Secret. Our people would be afraid to go without it. If we have it, Jack will take us to some island that he knows of across the seas. But we cannot go without the Secret. You shall bring it with you."

"When could we go?" he asked, whispering.

"We could go at any time—in a day—in a week—when you please. Oh, Harry, will you indeed rescue us? Will you come with us? Some of us are resolved to go—Secret or not. I am one of those. Will you let me go—alone?"

"Is it impossible," he said, "that you should go without the Secret?"

"Yes," she said; "the people would be afraid. But oh, to think of a new life, where we shall no longer be all the same, but different! Every one shall have his own possessions again—whatever he can win; every one his own profession; the women shall dress as they please; we shall have Art—and Music—and Poetry again. And—oh, Harry!"—she leaned her head upon his shoulder—"we shall have Love again. Oh, to think of it! Oh, to think of it! Love once more! And with Love, think of all the other things that will come back. *They must* come back, Harry— the old Faith which formerly made us happy—" Her voice choked, and she burst into tears.

I crouched behind the statues, listening. What did she cry about? The old Faith? She could have that if she wanted, I suppose, without crying over it. No law whatever against it.

Dr. Linister said nothing, but I saw that he was shaking—actually shaking—and trembling all over. A most remarkable person! Who would have believed that weakness so lamentable could lie behind so much science?

"I yield," he said—"I yield, Mildred. The Present is so horrible that it absolves me even from the most solemn oath. Love has been killed— we will revive it again. All the sweet and precious things that made life happy have been killed; Art and Learning and Music, all have been killed—we will revive them. Yes, I will go with you, my dear; and— since you cannot go without—I will bring the Secret with me."

"Oh, Harry! Harry!" She flung herself into his arms. "You have made me more happy than words can tell. Oh, you are mine—you are mine, and I am yours!"

"As for the Secret," he went on, "it belongs, if it is to be used at all, to all mankind. Why did the College of Physicians guard it in their own jealous keeping, save to make themselves into a mysterious and separate Caste? Must men always appoint sacred guardians of so-called mysteries which belong to all? My dear, since the Great Discovery, Man has been sinking lower and lower. He can go very little lower now. You have been rescued from the appalling fate which Grout calls the Triumph of Science. Yes—yes—" he repeated, as if uncertain, "the Secret belongs to all or none. Let all have it and work out their destiny in freedom, or let none have it, and so let us go back to the old times, when such great things were done against the fearful odds of so short and uncertain a span. Which would be the better?"

"Only come with us, my lover. Oh, can a simple woman make you happy? Come with us; but let our friends know—else they will not come with us—that whenever we go, we have the Secret."

"It belongs to all," he repeated. "Come with me, then, Mildred, to the House of Life. You shall be the first to whom the Secret shall be revealed. And you, if you please, shall tell it to all our friends. It is the Secret, and that alone, which keeps up the Authority of the College. Come. It is dark; but I have a key to the North Postern. Come with me. In the beginning of this new Life which lies before us, I will, if you wish, give the Secret to all who share it. Come, my Love, my Bride."

He led her by the hand quickly down the Picture Gallery and out into the Garden.

I looked round. The silly folk in the Museum were going on with their masquerade—laughing, singing, dancing. The girl Christine ran in and out among them with bright eyes and eager looks. And the eyes of the sailor, Jack Carera, followed her everywhere. Oh yes. I knew what those eyes meant—the old selfishness—the subjection of the Woman. She was to be his Property. And yet she seemed to like it. Forever and anon she made some excuse to pass him, and touched his hand as she passed and smiled sweetly. I dare say that she was a beautiful girl—but Beauty has nothing at all to do with the Administration of the people. However, there was no time to be lost. The Arch Physician was going to betray the Great Secret.

Happily he would have to go all the way round to the North Postern. There was time, if I was quick, to call witnesses, and to seize him in the very act. And then—the Penalty. Death! Death! Death!

IX

IN THE INNER HOUSE

The House of Life, you have already learned, is a great and venerable building. We build no such houses now. No one but those who belong to the Holy College—viz., the Arch Physician, the Suffragan, the Fellows or Physicians, and the Assistants—are permitted to enter its doors or to witness the work that is carried on within these walls. It is, however, very well understood that this work concerns the prolongation of the Vital Forces first, the preservation of Health next, and the enlargement of scientific truth generally. The House is, in fact, the great laboratory in which the Fellows conduct those researches of which it is not permitted to speak outside. The prevention of disease, the cure of hereditary and hitherto incurable diseases, the continual lowering of the hours of labor, by new discoveries in Chemistry and Physics, are now the principal objects of these researches. When, in fact, we have discovered how to provide food chemically out of simple matter, and thereby abolish the necessity for cultivation, no more labor will be required, and Humanity will have taken the last and greatest step of all—freedom from the necessity of toil. After that, there will be no more need for labor, none for thought, none for anxiety. At stated intervals food, chemically prepared, will be served out; between those intervals man will lie at rest—asleep, or in the torpor of unthinking rest. This will be, as I have said before, the Triumph of Science.

The House, within, is as magnificent as it is without; that is to say, it is spacious even beyond our requirements, and lofty even beyond the wants of a laboratory. All day long the Fellows and the Assistants work at their tables. Here is everything that Science wants—furnaces, electric batteries, retorts, instruments of all kinds, and collections of everything that may be wanted. Here—behind the Inner House—is a great workshop where our glass vessels are made, where our instruments are manufactured and repaired. The College contains two or three hundred of Assistants working in their various departments. These men, owing to the restlessness of their intellect, sometimes give trouble, either because they want to learn more than the Fellows think sufficient for them, or because they invent something unexpected, or because they become dissatisfied with the tranquil conditions of their life. Some of them from time to time have gone mad. Some, who threatened more trouble, have been painlessly extinguished.

Within the House itself is the Inner House, to enter which is forbidden, save to the Arch Physician, the Suffragan, and the Fellows.

This place is a kind of House within a House. Those who enter from the South Porch see before them, more than half-way up the immense building, steps, upon which stands a high screen of wood-work. This screen, which is very ancient, protects the Inner House from entrance or observation. It runs round the whole enclosure, and is most profusely adorned with carved-work representing all kinds of things. For my own part, I have never examined into the work, and I hardly know what it is that is here figured. What does it advance science to carve bunches of grapes (which everybody understands not to be grapes) in wood? All these things in the House of Life—the carved wood, the carved stone, the carved marble, the lofty pillars, the painted windows—irritate and offend me. Yet the Arch Physician, who loved to sit alone in the Inner House, would contemplate these works of Art with a kind of rapture. Nay, he would wellnigh weep at thinking that now there are no longer any who can work in that useless fashion.

As for what is within the Inner House, I must needs speak with caution. Suffice it, therefore, to say that round the sides of the screen are ancient carved seats under carved canopies, which are the seats of the Fellows; and that on a raised stone platform, approached by several steps, is placed the Coffer which contains the Secret of the Great Discovery. The Arch Physician alone had the key of the Coffer; he and his Suffragan alone possessed the Secret; the Fellows were only called into the Inner House when a Council was held on some new Discovery or some new adaptation of Science to the wants of Mankind.

Now, after overhearing the intended treason of the Arch Physician, and witnessing his degradation and fall, I made haste to act; for I plainly perceived that if the miraculous Prolongation of the Vital Force should be allowed to pass out of our own hands, and to become public property, an end would at once be put to the Order and Discipline now so firmly established; the Authority of the College would be trampled under foot; everybody would begin to live as they pleased; the old social conditions might be revived; and the old social inequalities would certainly begin again, because the strong would trample on the weak. This was, perhaps, what Dr. Linister designed. I remembered, now, how long it was before he could forget the old distinctions; nay, how impossible it was for him ever to bring himself to regard me, though his Suffragan—whom he had formerly made his serving-man—as his equal. Thinking of that time, and of those distinctions, strengthened my purpose. What I did and how I prevented the treachery will approve itself to all who have the best interests of mankind at heart.

THE HOUSE OF LIFE AFTER nightfall is very dark; the windows are high, for the most part narrow, and, though there are a great many of them, most are painted, so that even on a clear and bright day there is not more light than enough to carry on experiments, and, if I had my way, I would clear out all the painted glass. It is, of course, provided with the electric light; but this is seldom used except in the short and dark days of winter, when work is carried on after nightfall. In the evening the place is absolutely empty. John Lax, the Porter, occupies the South Porch and keeps the keys. But there is another and smaller door in the north transept. It leads to a Court of Cloisters, the ancient use of which has long been forgotten, the key of which is kept by the Arch Physician himself.

It was with this key—at this entrance—that he came into the House. He opened the door and closed it behind him. His footstep was not the only one; a lighter step was heard on the stones as well. In the silence of the place and time the closing of the door rumbled in the roof overhead like distant thunder, and the falling of the footsteps echoed along the walls of the great building.

The two companions did not speak.

A great many years ago, in the old times, there was a Murder done here—a foul murder by a band of soldiers, who fell upon a Bishop or Saint or Angel—I know not whom. The memory of the Murder has survived the name of the victim and the very religion which he professed—it was, perhaps, that which was still maintained among the aristocracy when I was a boy. Not only is the memory of the murder preserved, but John Lax—who, soon after the Great Discovery, when we took over the building from the priests of the old religion, was appointed its Porter and heard the old stories—would tell all those who chose to listen how the Murderers came in at that small door and how the murder was committed on such a spot, the stones of which are to this day red with the blood of the murdered man. On the spot, however, stands now a great electrical battery.

The Arch Physician, now about to betray his trust, led his companion, the woman Mildred Carera, by the hand past this place to the steps which lead to the Inner House. They ascended those steps. Standing there, still outside the Inner House, Dr. Linister bade the woman turn round and look upon the Great House of Life.

The clouds had dispersed, and the moonlight was now shining through the windows of the South, lighting up the colored glass, painting bright pictures and patterns upon the floor, and pouring white light through those windows, which are not painted, upon the clustered pillars and old monuments of the place. Those who were now gathered in the Inner House listened, holding their breath in silence.

"Mildred," said Dr. Linister, "long, long years ago we stood together upon this spot. It was after a Service of Praise and Prayer to the God whom then the world worshipped. We came from town with a party to see this Cathedral. When service was over, I scoffed at it in the light manner of the time, which questioned everything and scoffed at everything."

"I remember, Harry; and all through the service my mind was filled with—you."

"I scoff no more, Mildred. We have seen to what a depth men can sink when the Hope of the Future is taken from them. The memory of that service comes back to me, and seems to consecrate the place and the time. Mildred," he said, after a pause—oh, the House was very silent—"this is a solemn and a sacred moment for us both. Here, side by side, on the spot once sacred to the service of the God whom we have long forgotten, let us renew the vows which were interrupted so long ago. Mildred, with all my heart, with all my strength, I love thee."

"Harry," she murmured, "I am thine—even to Death itself."

"Even to Death itself," he replied. "Yes, if it comes to that. If the Great Discovery itself must be abandoned; if we find that only at that price can we regain the things we have lost."

"It was Grout who destroyed Religion—not the Great Discovery," said the girl.

We kept silence in the House, but we heard every word. And this was true, and my heart glowed to think how true it was.

"Nay, not Grout, nor a thousand Grouts. Without the certainty of parting, Religion droops and dies. There must be something not understood, something unknown, beyond our power of discovery, or the dependence which is the ground of religion dies away in man's heart. He who is immortal and commands the secrets of Nature, so that he shall neither die, nor grow old, nor become feeble, nor fall into any disease, feels no necessity for any religion. This House, Mildred, is the expression of religion at the time of man's greatest dependence. To the God in whom, short-lived, ignorant, full of disease, he trusted he built this splendid place, and put into it all the beauty that he could command of sculpture and of form. But it speaks no longer to the People for whom it was built. When the Great Discovery was made, it would surely have been better to have found out whither it was going to lead us before we consented to receive it."

"Surely—" said Mildred, but the other interrupted her.

"We did not understand; we were blind—we were blind."

"Yet—we live."

"And you have just now told me how. Remember the things that men said when the Discovery was made. We were to advance continually; we were to scale heights hitherto unapproached; we were to achieve things hitherto unknown in Art as well as in Science. Was it for the Common Meal, the Common Dress, the Common Toil, the vacant face, the lips that never smile, the eyes that never brighten, the tongue that never speaks, the heart that beats only for itself, that we gave up the things we had?"

"We did not expect such an end, Harry."

"No; we had not the wit to expect it. Come, Mildred, I will give you the Secret, and you may give it, if you please, to all the world. Oh, I feel as if the centuries had fallen away! I am full of hope again. I am full of the old life once more; and, Mildred—oh, my sweet!—I am full of Love!"

He stooped and kissed her on the lips. Then he led her into the Inner House.

Now, JUST BEFORE DR. LINISTER TURNED the key of the postern, the door of the South Porch was softly closed, and a company of twenty men walked lightly and noiselessly, in slippers, up the nave of the House. Arrived at the Inner House, they ascended the steps and entered that dark Chapel, every man making straight for his own seat and taking it without a word or a breath. This was the College of Physicians hastily called by me, and gathered together to witness the Great Treachery of the Chief. They sat there silent and breathless listening to their talk.

THE SECRET WAS KEPT IN a cipher, intelligible only to the two who then guarded it, in a fire-proof chest upon the stone table which was once the altar of the old Faith.

Dr. Linister stood before the chest, his key in his hand.

"It would be better," he said, "if the new departure could be made without the Secret. It would be far, far better if we could start again under the old conditions; but if they are afraid to go without the Secret, why—" He unlocked the chest. Then he paused again.

"How many years have I been the guardian of this Secret? Mildred, when I think of the magnificent vistas which opened up before our eyes when this Great Discovery was made; when I think of the culture without bound or limit; the Art in which the hand was always to grow more and more dexterous; the Science which was to advance with gigantic strides—my child, I feel inclined to sink into the earth with shame, only to compare that dream with the awful, the terrible, the disgraceful reality! Let us all go away. Let us leave this place, and let us make a new beginning, with sadder minds, yet with this experience of the Present to guide us and to keep us from committing worse follies. See, dear—here is the Secret. The cipher in which it is written has a key which is in this paper. I place all in your hands. If accident should destroy me, you have the Secret still for yourself and friends. Use it well—use it better than we have used it. Kiss me, Mildred. Oh, my dear!"

Then, as they lay in each other's arms, I turned on the electric light and discovered them. The chest stood open; the papers, cipher, key and all, were in the girl's hands; the Arch Physician was caught in the very act of his supreme Treachery!

And lo! the Fellows of the Holy College were in the Inner House; every man in his place, every man looking on, and every man standing upright with eyes and gestures of scorn.

"Traitor!" they cried, one and all.

John Lax appeared at the door, halberd in hand.

X

The Council in the House

Brothers of the Holy College!" I cried, "you have beheld the crime—you are witnesses of the Fact—you have actually seen the Arch Physician himself revealing the Great Secret, which none of yourselves, even of the College, hath been permitted to learn—the Secret confined by the Wisdom of the College to himself and to his Suffragan."

"We are witnesses," they cried, with one consent. To my great satisfaction, even those who were of Dr. Linister's party, and who voted with him against the Administration and Policy of the College, spoke, on this occasion, for the plain and undeniable truth.

"What," I asked, "is the Penalty when one of the least among us, even an Assistant only, betrays to the People any of the secrets—even the least secret—of the work carried on in this House?"

"It is DEATH," they replied, with one voice.

"It is DEATH," I repeated, pointing to the Arch Physician.

At such a moment, when nothing short of annihilation appeared in view, one would have expected from the guilty pair an appearance of the greatest consternation and dismay. On the contrary, the Arch Physician, with an insensibility—or a bravado—which one would not have expected of him, stood before us all, his arms folded, his eyes steady, his lips even smiling. Beside him stood the girl, dressed in the ridiculous mummery of the nineteenth century, bowed down, her face in her hands.

"It is I," she murmured—"it is I, Harry, who have brought you to this. Oh, forgive me! Let us die together. Since I have awakened out of the stupid torpor of the Present—since we remembered the Past—and Love—let us die together; for I could not live without you." She knelt at his feet, and laid her head upon his arm. "My love," she said, "my Lord and Love! let me die with you."

At this extraordinary spectacle I laughed aloud. Love? I thought the old wives' tales of Love and Lordship were long, long since dead and forgotten. Yet here was a man for the sake of a woman—actually because she wanted to go away and begin again the old pernicious life—breaking his most sacred vows; and here was a woman—for the sake of this man—actually and truly for his sake—asking for death—death with him! Since, when they were both dead, there could be no more any feeling one for the other, why ask for death? What good could that do for either?

"Your wish," I said to this foolish woman, "shall be gratified, in case the Judges of your case decide that your crime can be expiated by no less a penalty. Fellows of the College, let this guilty pair be confined for the night, and to-morrow we will try them solemnly in the College Court according to ancient custom."

I know not how many years had elapsed since that Court was held. The offences of the old time were for the most part against property—since there had been no property, there had been no crimes of this kind. Another class of old offences consisted of violence rising out of quarrels; since almost all these quarrels originated in disputes about property—every man in the old time who had property was either a thief or the son of a thief, so that disputes were naturally incessant—there could be no longer any such quarrels or any such violence. A third class of crimes were caused by love, jealousy, and the like; these two had happily, as we believed, disappeared forever.

The last class of crimes to vanish were those of mutiny. When the People grew gradually to understand that the welfare of all was the only rule of the governing body, and that selfishness, individualism, property, privilege, would no longer be permitted, they left off murmuring, and mutiny ceased. You have seen how orderly, how docile, how tranquil, is the life of the People as it has been ordered by the Sacred College. Alas! I thought that this order, this sheep-like freedom from Thought, was going to be henceforth universal and undisturbed.

Our prisoners made no opposition. John Lax, the Porter, bearing his halberd of office, marched beside them. We closed in behind them, and in this order we led them to the strong room over the South Porch, which is provided with bars and a lock. It is the sleeping-chamber of John Lax, but for this night he was to remain on the watch below.

Then, as Suffragan, I called a Council of Emergency in the Inner House, taking the Presidency in the absence of the Arch Physician.

I told my brethren briefly what had happened; how my attention had been called to the fact that a company of the People, headed by the young girl called Christine, had begun to assemble every night in the Museum, there to put on clothes which belonged to the old time, and to masquerade in the manners, language, and amusements (so called) of that time; that this assemblage, which might have been innocent and even laudable if it led, as it should have done, to a detestation of the old times, had proved mischievous, because, strangely enough, it had exactly the opposite effect; that, in fact, everybody in the company had fallen into an ardent yearning after the Past, and that all the bad features of that bad time—the Social inequality, the Poverty, the Injustice—were carefully ignored.

Upon this, one of Dr. Linister's Party arose, and begged permission to interrupt the Suffragan. He wished to point out that memory was indestructible; that even if we succeeded in reducing Mankind, as the Suffragan wished, to be a mere breathing and feeding machine—the Ultimate Triumph of Science—any one of these machines might be at any time electrified into a full and exact memory of the Past; that, to the average man, the Emotion of the Past would always be incomparably preferable to the Tranquillity of the Present. What had just been done would be done again.

I went on, after this interruption, to narrate how I set myself to watch, and presently saw the Arch Physician himself enter the Museum; how he exchanged his gown for the costume in which the men disfigured themselves, play-acted, pretended, and masqueraded with them; danced with them, no external respect whatever being paid to his rank; and afterwards had certain love passages—actually love passages between the Arch Physician and a Woman of the People!—which I overheard, and repeated as far as I could remember them. The rest my brethren of the College knew already; how I hastily summoned them, and led them into the Inner House just before the arrival of the Criminals.

Thereupon, without any attempt of Dr. Linister's friends to the contrary, it was Resolved that the Trial of the Arch Physician and his accomplices should be held in the morning.

I next invited their attention to the behavior of the girl Christine. She it was, I told them, who had instigated the whole of the business. A culpable curiosity it was, no doubt, that first led her to consider and study the ways of the ancient world; what should be the ways of the Past to an honest and loyal person, satisfied with the Wisdom which ruled the Present? She read the old books, looked at the old pictures, and lived all day long in the old Museum. There were many things which she could not understand; she wanted to understand these things; and she conceived a violent, unreasoning admiration for the old time, which appeared to this foolish girl to be a continual round of pleasure and excitement. Therefore she gathered together a company of those who had belonged to the richer class in the days when property was permitted. She artfully awakened them out of their contentment, sowed the seeds of dissatisfaction among them, caused them to remember the Past with a vehement longing to reproduce the worst part of it—namely, the manners and customs of the richer class—the people for whom the bulk of mankind toiled, so that the privileged few might have nothing to do but to feast, dance, sing, and make love. I asked the College, therefore, what should be done with such a girl, warning them that one Penalty, and one only, would meet the case and render for the future such outbreaks impossible.

Again the Physician who had spoken before rose up and remarked that such outbreaks were inevitable, because the memory is indestructible.

"You have here," he said, "a return to the Past, because a young girl, by reading the old books, has been able to stimulate the memory of those who were born in the Past. Other things may bring about the same result; a dream, the talking together of two former friends. Let the girl alone. She has acted as we might have expected a young girl—the only young girl among us—to have acted. She has found that the Past, which some of us have represented as full of woe and horror, had its pleasant side; she asks why that pleasant side could not be reproduced. I, myself, or any of us, might ask the same question. Nay, it is well known that I protest—and always shall protest, my friends and I—against the Theory of the Suffragan. His Triumph of Science we consider horrible to the last degree. I, for one, shall never be satisfied until the Present is wholly abolished, and until we have gone back to the good old system of Individualism, and begun to encourage the People once more to cultivate the old happiness by the old methods of their own exertion."

I replied that my own recollection of the old time was perfectly clear, and that there was nothing but unhappiness in it. As a child I lived in the street; I never had enough to eat; I was cuffed and kicked; I could never go to bed at night until my father, who always came home drunk, was asleep; the streets were full of miserable children like myself. Where was the happiness described by my learned brother? Where was the pleasant side? More I said, but it suffices to record that by a clear majority it was Resolved to arrest the girl Christine in the morning, and to try all three prisoners, as soon as the Court could be prepared for them, according to ancient usage.

Early in the morning I sought an interview with the Arch Physician.

WALTER BESANT

I found him, with the woman Mildred, sitting in the Chamber over the Porch. There was no look of terror, or even of dejection, on the face of either. Rather there was an expression as of exaltation. Yet they were actually going to die—to cease breathing—to lose consciousness!

I told the prisoner that I desired to represent my own conduct in its true light. I reminded him that, with him, I was guardian of the Holy Secret. The power and authority of the College, I pointed out, were wholly dependent upon the preservation of that Secret in its own hands. By divulging it to the People he would make them as independent of the Physician as the Great Discovery itself had made them independent of the Priest. The latter had, as he pretended, the Keys of the After Life. The former did actually hold those of the Actual Life. The authority of the Physician gone, the people would proceed to divide among themselves, to split up into factions, to fight and quarrel, to hold private property, and in fact would speedily return to the old times, and all the work that we had accomplished would be destroyed. Every man would have the knowledge of the Secret for himself and his family. They would all begin to fight again—first for the family, next for the Commune, and then for the tribe or nation. All this would have been brought about by his treachery had not I prevented it.

"Yes," he said, "doubtless you are quite right, Grout." He spoke quite in the old manner, as if I had been still his servant in the old laboratory. It was not till afterwards that I remembered this, and became enraged to think of his arrogance. "We will not argue the matter. It is not worth while. You acted after your kind, and as I might have expected." Again it was not until afterwards that I considered what he meant and was enraged. "When we allowed gentlehood to be destroyed, gentle manners, honor, dignity, and such old virtues went too. You acted—for yourself—very well, Grout. Have you anything more to say? As for us, we have gone back to the old times, this young lady and I—quite to the old, old times." He took her hand and kissed it, while his eyes met hers, and they were filled with a tenderness which amazed me. "This lady, Grout," he said, "has done me the honor of accepting my hand. You will understand that no greater happiness could have befallen me. The rest that follows is of no importance—none—not the least. My dear, this is Grout, formerly employed in my laboratory. Unfortunately he has no experience of Love, or of any of the Arts or Culture of the good old Time; but a man of great intelligence. You can go, Grout."

XI

The Trial and Sentence

I was greatly pleased with the honest zeal shown by John Lax, the Porter, on this occasion. When, after snatching three or four hours' sleep, I repaired to the House, I found that worthy creature polishing at a grindstone nothing less than a great, heavy Execution Axe, which had done service many times in the old, old days on Tower Hill, and had since peacefully reposed in the Museum.

"Suffragan," he said, "I am making ready." His feet turned the treadle, and the wheel flew round, and the sparks showered from the blunt old weapon. He tried the edge with his finger. "'Tis not so sharp as a razor," he said, "but 'twill serve."

"John Lax, methinks you anticipate the sentence of the Court."

"Suffragan, with submission, it is Death to divulge any secret of this House. It is Death even for me, Porter of the House, to tell them outside of any Researches or Experiments that I may observe in my service about the House. And if so great a Penalty is pronounced against one who would reveal such trifles as I could divulge, what of the Great Secret itself?"

"Lax, you are a worthy man. Know, therefore, that this Secret once divulged, the Authority of the College would vanish; and we, even the Physicians themselves—to say nothing of the Assistants, the Bedells, and you yourself—would become no better than the Common People. You do well to be zealous."

John Lax nodded his head. He was a taciturn man habitually; but now he became loquacious. He stopped the grindstone, laid down the axe, and rammed his hands into his pockets.

"When I see them women dressed up like swells—" he began, grinning.

"John, this kind of language belongs to the old days, when even speech was unequal."

"No matter; you understand it. Lord! Sammy Grout, the brewer's boy—we were both Whitechapel pets; but I was an old 'un of five and thirty, while you were on'y beginning to walk the Waste with a gal on your arm—p'r'aps—and a ha'penny fag in your mouth. Hold on, now. It's like this—"

What with the insolence of Dr. Linister, and the sight of the old dresses, and the sound of the old language, I myself was carried away. Yes, I was once more Sam Grout; again I walked upon the pavement of the Whitechapel Road; again I was a boy in the great brewery of Mile End Road.

"Go on, John Lax," I said, with condescension. "Revive, if it is possible, something of the Past. I give you full leave. But when you come to the Present, forget not the reverence due to the Suffragan."

"Right, guv'nor. Well, then, it's like this. I see them men and women dressed up in the old fallals, and goin' on like I've seen 'em goin' on long ago with their insolence and their haw-haws—damn 'em—and all the old feelings came back to me, and I thought I was spoutin' again on a Sunday mornin', and askin' my fellow-countrymen if they always meant to sit down and be slaves. And the memory came back to me—ah! proper it did—of a speech I made 'em one mornin' all about this French Revolution. 'Less 'ave our own Revolution,' I sez, sez I. 'Less bring out all the Bloomin' Kings and Queens,' I sez, 'the Dukes and Markisses, the fat Bishops and the lazy Parsons. Less do what the French did. Less make 'em shorter by the 'ed,' I sez. That's what I said that mornin'. Some of the people laughed, and some of 'em went away. There never was a lot more difficult to move than them Whitechappellers. They'd listen—and then they'd go away. They'd too much fine speeches give 'em—that was the matter with 'em—too much. Nothing never came of it. That night I was in the Public havin' a drop, and we began to talk. There was a row, and a bit of a fight. But before we was fired out I up and said plain, for everybody to hear, that when it came to choppin' off their noble 'eds I'd be the man to do it—and joyful, I said. Well now, Sammy Grout, you were in that Public Bar among that crowd—maybe you've forgotten it. But I remember you very well. You was standin' there, and you laughed about the choppin'. You've forgotten, Sammy. Think. It was a fine summer evenin': you weren't in Church. Come now—you can't say you ever went to Church, Sammy Grout."

"I never did. But go on, John Lax. Recall as much of the Past as you wish, if it makes you love the Present more. I would not say aught to diminish an honest zeal."

"Right, guv'nor. Well, I never got that chance. There was no choppin' of 'eds at all. When we had to murder the old people, your Honor would have it done scientifically; and there was as many old working-men killed off as swells, which was a thousand pities, an' made a cove's heart bleed. What I say is this. Here we've got a return to the old Times. Quite unexpected it is. Now we've got such a chance, which will never come again, let 'em just see how the old Times worked. Have a Procession, with the Executioner goin' before the criminals, his axe on his shoulder ready to begin. If you could only be Sammy Grout again—but that can't be, I'm afraid—what a day's outing you would have had to be sure! Suffragan, let us show 'em how the old Times worked. And let me be the Executioner. I'll do it, I promise you, proper. I've got the old spirit upon me—ah! and the old strength, too—just as I had then. Oh! It's too much!" He sat down and hugged the axe. I thought he would have kissed it. "It's too much! To think that the time would ever come when I should execute a swell—and that swell the Arch Physician himself. Damn him! He's always looked as if everybody else was dirt beneath his feet."

"I know not," I told him gently, "what may be the decision of the Court. But, John Lax, continue to grind your axe. I would not throw cold water on honest zeal. Your strength, you say, is equal to your spirit. You will not flinch at the last moment. Ah! we have some honest men left."

The Court was held that morning in the nave of the House itself. The Judges, who were the whole College of Physicians, sat in a semicircle; whereas the three prisoners stood in a row—the Arch Physician carrying himself with a haughty insolence which did not assist his chances: clinging to his arm, still in her silk dress, with her bracelets and chains, and her hair artfully arranged, was the woman called Mildred. She looked once, hurriedly, at the row of Judges, and then turned with a shudder—she found small comfort in those faces—to her lover, and laid her head upon his shoulder, while he supported her with his arm. The degradation and folly of the Arch Physician, apart from the question of his guilt, as shown in this behavior, were complete.

Beside Mildred stood the girl Christine. Her face was flushed; her eyes were bright: she stood with clasped hands, looking steadily at the Judges: she wore, instead of the Regulation Dress, a frock of white stuff, which she had found, I suppose, in the Museum—as if open disobedience of our laws would prove a passport to favor. She had let her long hair fall upon her shoulders and down her back. Perhaps she hoped to conquer her Judges by her beauty—old time phrase! Woman's beauty, indeed, to Judges who know every bone and every muscle in woman's body, and can appreciate the nature of her intellect, as well as of her structure! Woman's Beauty! As if that could ever again move the world!

Behind the President's Chair—I was the President—stood John Lax, bearing his halberd of office.

The Doors of the House were closed: the usual sounds of Laboratory work were silent: the Assistants, who usually at this hour would have been engaged in Research and Experiment, were crowded outside the Court.

I have been told, since, that there were omitted at the Trial many formalities which should have been observed at such a Trial. For instance, there should have been a Clerk or two to make notes of the proceedings: there should have been a Formal Indictment: and there should have been Witnesses. But these are idle forms. The guilt of the Prisoners was proved: we had seen it with our own eyes. We were both Judges and Witnesses.

I was once, however, in the old days, charged (and fined) before a magistrate in Bow Street for assaulting a Constable, and therefore I know something of how a Criminal Court should proceed. So, without any unnecessary formalities, I conducted the Trial according to Common Sense.

"What is your name?" I asked the Arch Physician.

"Harry Linister—once M.D. of Cambridge, and Fellow of the Royal Society."

"What are you by trade?"

"Physicist and Arch Physician of the Holy College of the Inner House."

"We shall see how long you will be able to describe yourself by those titles. Female Prisoner—you in the middle—what is your name?"

"I am the Lady Mildred Carera, daughter of the Earl of Thordisá."

"Come—come—none of your Ladyships and Earls here. We are now all equal. You are plain Mildred. And yours—you girl in the white frock? How dare you, either of you, appear before us in open violation of the Rules?"

"I am named Christine," she replied. "I have put on the white frock because it is becoming."

At this point I was interrupted by a whisper from John Lax.

"Christine's friends," he said, "are gathering in the Museum, and they are very noisy. They threaten to give trouble."

"When the Trial and Execution are over," I told him, "arrest them every one. Let them all be confined in the Museum. To-morrow, or perhaps this afternoon, we will try them as well."

The man grinned with satisfaction. Had he known what a fatal mistake I was making, he would not have grinned. Rather would his face have expressed the most dreadful horror.

Then the Trial proceeded.

"Dr. Linister," I said, "it is a very singular point in this case that we have not to ask you whether you plead 'guilty' or 'not guilty,' because we have all seen you with our own eyes engaged in the very act with which you are charged. You *are* guilty."

"I am," he replied, calmly.

"Your companion is also guilty. I saw her practising upon you those blandishments, or silly arts, by which women formerly lured men. We also saw her on the point of receiving from you the Great Secret, which must never be suffered to leave this Building."

"Yes," she said, "if he is guilty, I am guilty as well."

"As for you" (I turned to Christine), "you have been so short a time in the world—only nineteen years or so—that to leave it will cause little pain to you. It is not as if you had taken root with all the years of life which the others have enjoyed. Yet the Court would fail in its duty did it not point out the enormity of your offence. You were allowed to grow up undisturbed in the old Museum: you spent your time in developing a morbid curiosity into the Past. You were so curious to see with your own eyes what it was to outward show, that you cast about to find among the tranquil and contented People some whose minds you might disturb and lead back to the restless old times. This was a most guilty breach of confidence. Have you anything to say? Do you confess?"

"Yes, I confess."

"Next, you, with this woman and a Company who will also be brought to Justice before long, began to assemble together, and to revive, with the assistance of books, pictures, dress, and music, a portion of the Past. But what portion? Was it the portion of the vast majority, full of disease, injustice, and starvation? Did you show how the old Times filled the houses with struggling needlewomen and men who refused to struggle any longer? Did you show the Poor and the Unemployed? Not at all. You showed the life of the Rich and the Idle. And so you revived a longing for what shall never—never—be permitted to return—the Period of Property and the Reign of Individualism. It was your crime to misrepresent the Past, and to set forth the Exception as the Rule. This must be made impossible for the future. What have you to say, Christine?"

"Nothing. I told you before. Nothing. I have confessed. Why keep on asking me?"

She looked round the Court with no apparent fear. I suppose it was because she was so young, and had not yet felt any apprehension of the Fate which was now so near unto her.

"Dr. Linister," I said, "before considering its sentence, the Court will hear what you may have to say."

"I have but little to say," he replied. "Everybody in the College knows that I have always been opposed to the methods adopted by the Suffragan and the College. During the last few days, however, I have been enabled to go back once more to the half-forgotten Past, and have experienced once more the Emotions of which you have robbed Life. I have seen once more, after many, many years, the Fighting Passion, the Passion of Private Rights, and"—his voice dropped to a whisper—"I have experienced once more the Passion of Love." He stooped and kissed the woman Mildred on the forehead. "I regret that we did not succeed. Had we not been caught, we should by this time have been beyond your power—the Secret with us, to use or not, as we pleased—with a company strong enough to defy you, and with the old Life again before us, such as we enjoyed before you robbed us of it. We should have welcomed the old Life, even under the old conditions: we welcome, instead of it, the Thing which, only to think of, makes your hearts almost to stop beating with fear and horror."

He stopped. That was a speech likely to win indulgence from the Court, was it not?

I turned to the woman Mildred.

"And you?" I asked.

"What have I to say? The Present I loathe—I loathe—I loathe. I would not go back to it if you offered me instant release with that condition. I have found Love. Let me die—let me die—let me die!"

She clung to her lover passionately, weeping and sobbing. He soothed her and caressed her. John Lax, behind me, snorted.

Then I asked the girl Christine what she wished to say.

She laughed—she actually laughed.

"Oh!" she said, "in return for the past weeks, there is no punishment which I would not cheerfully endure. We have had—oh! the most delightful time. It has been like a dream. Oh! Cruel, horrid, wicked men! You found such a Life in the old Time, and you destroyed it; and what have you given us in return? You have made us all equal who were born unequal. Go, look at the sad and heavy faces of the People. You have taken away everything, deliberately. You have destroyed all—all. You have left nothing worth living for. Why, I am like Mildred. I would not go back to the Present again if I could! Yes, for one thing I would—to try and raise a Company of Men—not sheep—and hound them on to storm this place, and to kill—yes, to kill"—the girl looked so dangerous that any thought of mercy was impossible—"every one who belongs to this Accursed House of Life!"

Here was a pretty outcome of study in the Museum! Here was a firebrand let loose among us straight from the bad old Nineteenth Century! And we had allowed this girl actually to grow up in our very midst.

Well, she finished, and stood trembling with rage, cheeks burning, eyes flashing—a very fury.

I invited the Court to retire to the Inner House, and took their opinions one by one.

They were unanimous on several points—first, that the position of things was most dangerous to the Authority of the College and the safety of the People; next, that the punishment of Death alone would meet the case; thirdly, that, in future, the Museum, with the Library and Picture Galleries, must be incorporated with the College itself, so that this danger of the possible awakening of memory should be removed.

Here, however, our unanimity ceased. For the Fellow, of whom I have already spoken as having always followed the Arch Physician, arose and again insisted that what had happened to-day might very well happen again: that nothing was more uncertain in its action, or more indestructible, than human memory: so that, from time to time, we must look for the arising of some Leader or Prophet who would shake up the people and bring them out of their torpor to a state of discontent and yearning after the lost. Wherefore he exhorted us to reconsider our Administration, and to provide some safety-valve for the active spirits. As to the Death of the three criminals, he would not, he could not, oppose it. He proposed, however, that the mode of Death should be optional. So great a light of Science as the Arch Physician had many secrets, and could doubtless procure himself sudden and painless death if he chose. Let him have that choice for himself and his companions; and, as regards the girl, let her be cast into a deep sleep, and then painlessly smothered by gas, without a sentence being pronounced upon her at all. This leniency, he said, was demanded by her youth and her inexperience.

In reply, I pointed out that, as regards our Administration, we were not then considering it at all: that as for the mode of punishment, he had not only to consider the criminals, but also the People, and the effect of the Punishment upon them: we were not only to punish, but also to deter. I therefore begged the Court to go back to one of the former methods, and to one of the really horrible and barbarous, yet comparatively painless, methods. I showed that a mere report or announcement, made in the Public Hall, that the Arch Physician had been executed for Treason, would produce little or no effect upon the public mind, even if it were added that the two women, Mildred and Christine, had suffered with him: that our people needed to see the thing itself, in order to feel its true horror and to remember it. If Death alone were wanted, I argued, there were dozens of ways in which Life might be painlessly extinguished. But it was not Death alone that we desired; it was Terror that we wished to establish, in order to prevent another such attempt.

"Let them," I concluded, "be taken forth in solemn Procession to the open space before the Public Hall; we ourselves will form part of that Procession. Let them in that place, in the sight of all the People, be publicly decapitated by the Porter of the House, John Lax."

There was a good deal of opposition, at first, to this proposition, because it seemed barbarous and cruel; but the danger which had threatened the Authority—nay, the very existence—of the College, caused the opposition to give way. Why, if I had not been on the watch, the Secret would have been gone: the College would have been ruined. It was due to me that my proposals should be accepted. The sentence was agreed upon.

I am bound to confess that, on being brought back to receive the sentence of the Court, the Prisoners behaved with unexpected Fortitude. The male criminal turned pale, but only for a moment, and the two women caught each other by the hand. But they offered no prayer for mercy.

They were led back to their prison in the South Porch, until the necessary Preparations could be made.

XII

The Rebels

I t is useless to regret a thing that is done and over; otherwise one might very bitterly regret two or three steps in these proceedings. At the same time, it may be argued that what happened was the exact opposite of what we had every reason to expect, and therefore we could not blame ourselves with the event. After uncounted years of blind obedience, respect for authority, and unquestioning submission, had we not a full right to expect a continuance of the same spirit? What we did not know or suspect was the violence of the reaction that had set in. Not only had these revolutionaries gone back to the Past, but to the very worst traditions of the Past. They had not only become anxious to restore these old traditions; they had actually become men of violence, and were ready to back up their new convictions by an appeal to arms. We ought to have arrested the conspirators as soon as they assembled; we ought to have locked them up in the Museum and starved them into submission; we ought to have executed our criminals in private; in short, we ought to have done just exactly what we did not do.

While the Trial was proceeding, the new Party of Disorder were, as John Lax reported, gathered together in the Museum, considering what was best to be done.

They now knew all. When John Lax, in the morning, arrested the girl Christine, by my orders, he told her in plain language what had already happened.

"The Arch Physician is a Prisoner," he said. "He has been locked up all night in my room, over the South Porch. I watched below. Ha! If he had tried to escape, my instructions were to knock him on the head, Arch Physician or not. The woman Mildred is a Prisoner, as well. She was locked up with him. They may hold each other's hands and look into each other's eyes, in my room, as much as they please. And now, young woman, it is your turn."

"Mine?"

"Yours, my gal. So march along o' me."

"Why, what have I done that I should be arrested?"

"That you shall hear. March, I say. You are my Prisoner. You will stand your Trial—ah!" He smacked his lips to show his satisfaction, and wagged his head. He was a true Child of the People, and could not conceal his gratification at the discomfiture of traitors. "You will hear what the Court has to say—ah!" Again he repeated this sign of satisfaction. "You will be tried, and you will hear the Sentence of the Court—ah, ah! Do you know what it will be? Death!" he whispered. "Death for all! I see the sentence in the Suffragan's face. Oh! he means it."

The girl heard without reply; but her cheeks turned pale.

"You won't mind much," he went on. "You hardly know what it is to live. You haven't been alive long enough to feel what it means. You're only a chit of a girl. If it wasn't for the example, I dare say they would let you off. But they won't—they won't. Don't try it on. Don't think of going on your knees, or anything else. Don't go weeping or crying. The Court is as hard as nails."

The honest fellow said this in his zeal for justice, and in the hope that nothing should be said or done which might avert just punishment. Otherwise, had this girl, who was, after all, young and ignorant, thrown herself fully and frankly upon our mercy, perhaps—I do not say—some of us might have been disposed to spare her. As it was—but you have seen.

"We waste time," he said. "March!"

She was dressed, as I have already related, in a masquerade white dress of the old time, with I know not what of ribbon round her waist, and wore her hair floating down her back.

The old man—her grandfather, as she called him—sat in his arm-chair, looking on and coughing. John Lax paid no attention to him at all.

"Good-by, grandad," she said, kissing him. "You will not see me any more, because they are going to kill me. You will find your inhaler in its place; but I am afraid you will have to manage for the future without any help. No one helps anybody in this beautiful Present. They are going to kill me. Do you understand? Poor old man! Good-by!"

She kissed him again and walked away with John Lax through the Picture Gallery, and so into the College Gardens, and by the north postern into the House of Life.

WHEN SHE WAS GONE THE old man looked about him feebly. Then he began to understand what had happened. His grandchild, the nurse and stay of his feebleness, was gone from him. She was going to be killed.

He was reckoned a very stupid old man always. To keep the cases in the Museum free from dust was all that he could do. But the revival of the Past acted upon him as it had acted upon the others: it took him out of his torpor and quickened his perceptions.

"Killed?" he cried. "My grandchild to be killed?"

He was not so stupid as not to know that there were possible protectors for her, if he could find them in time. Then he seized his stick and hurried as fast as his tottering limbs would carry him to the nearest field, where he knew the sailor, named John, or Jack, Carera, was employed for the time among the peas and beans.

"Jack Carera!" he cried, looking wildly about him and flourishing with his stick. "Jack! they are going to kill her! Jack—Jack Carera!—I say," he repeated. "Where is Jack Carera? Call him, somebody. They are going to kill her! They have taken my child a prisoner to the House of Life. I say Jack—Jack! Where is he? Where is he?"

The men were working in gangs. Nobody paid the least heed to the old man. They looked up, saw an old man—his hat blown off, his long white hair waving in the wind—brandishing wildly his stick, and shrieking for Jack. Then they went on with their work; it was no business of theirs. Docile, meek, and unquestioning are the People.

By accident, however, Jack was within hearing, and presently ran across the field.

"What is it?" he cried. "What has happened?"

"They have taken prisoner," the old man gasped, "the—the—Arch Physician—and—Lady Mildred—They are going to try them to-day before the College of Physicians. And now they have taken my girl—my Christine—and they will try her too. They will try them all, and they will kill them all."

"That shall be seen," said Jack, a fierce look in his eyes. "Go back to the Museum, old man, and wait for me. Keep quiet, if you can: wait for me."

In half an hour he had collected together the whole of the company, men and women, which formed their Party. They were thirty in number, and they came in from work in the Regulation Dress.

The sailor briefly related what had happened.

"Now," he said, "before we do anything more, let us put on the dress of the nineteenth century. That will help us to remember that our future depends upon ourselves, and will put heart in us."

This done, he made them a speech.

First, he reminded them how, by the help of one girl alone, the memory of the Past had been restored to them; next, he bade them keep in their minds the whole of that Past—every portion of it—and to brace up their courage with the thought of it—how delightful and desirable it was. And then he exhorted them to think of the Present, which he called loathsome, shameful, vile, and other bad names.

"We are in the gravest crisis of our fortunes," he concluded. "On our action this day depends our whole future. Either we emerge from this crisis free men and women, or we sink back into the Present, dull and dismal, without hope and without thought. Nay, there is more. If we do not rescue ourselves, we shall be very speedily finished off by the College. Do you think they will ever forgive us? Not so. As they deal with the Arch Physician and these two ladies, so they will deal with us. Better so. Better a thousand times to suffer Death at once, than to fall back into that wretched condition to which we were reduced. What! You, who have learned once more what is meant by Love, will you give that up? Will you give up these secret assemblies where we revive the glorious Past, and feel again the old thoughts and the old ambitions? Never—swear with me—never! never! never!"

They shouted together; they waved their hands; they were resolved. The men's eyes were alive again; in short, they were back again to the Past of their young days.

"First," said Jack, "let us arm."

He led them to a part of the Museum where certain old weapons stood stacked. Thanks to the Curator and to Christine, they had been kept bright and clear from rust by the application of oil.

"Here are swords, lances, rifles—but we have no ammunition—bayonets. Let us take the rifles and bayonets. So. To every man one. Now, the time presses. The Trial is going on. It may be too late in a few minutes to save the prisoners. Let us resolve."

Two plans suggested themselves at once. The first of these was to rush before the House of Life, break open the gates, and tear the prisoners from the hands of the Judges. The next was to ascertain, somehow, what was being done. The former counsel prevailed, and the men were already making ready for the attack when the great Bell of the House began to toll solemnly.

"What is that?" cried the women, shuddering.

It went on tolling, at regular intervals of a quarter of a minute. It was the knell for three persons about to die.

Then the doors of the South Porch flew open, and one of the Bedells came forth.

"What does that mean?" they asked.

The Bedell walked across the great Garden and began to ring the Bell of the Public Hall—the Dinner Bell.

Instantly the People began to flock in from the workshops and the fields, from all quarters, in obedience to a summons rarely issued. They flocked in slowly, and without the least animation, showing not the faintest interest in the proceedings. No doubt there was something or other—it mattered not what—ordered by the College.

"Go, somebody," cried Jack—"go, Hilda," he turned to one of the girls; "slip on your working dress; run and find out what is being done. Oh! if we are too late, they shall pay—they shall pay! Courage, men! Here are fifteen of us, well-armed and stout. We are equal to the whole of that coward mob. Run, Hilda, run!"

Hilda pushed her way through the crowd.

"What is it?" she asked the Bedell, eagerly. "What has happened?"

"You shall hear," he replied. "The most dreadful thing that can happen—a thing that has not happened since— . . . But you will hear."

He waited a little longer, until all seemed to be assembled. Then he stood upon a garden-bench and lifted up his voice:

"Listen! listen! listen!" he cried. "By order of the Holy College, listen! Know ye all that, for his crimes and treacheries, the Arch Physician has been deposed from his sacred office. Know ye all that he is condemned to die." There was here a slight movement—a shiver—as of a wood, on a still autumn day, at the first breath of the wind. "He is condemned to die. He will be brought out without delay, and will be executed in the sight of the whole People." Here they trembled. "There are also condemned with him, as accomplices in his guilt, two women—named respectively Mildred, or Mildred Carera in the old style, and the girl Christine. Listen! listen! listen! It is forbidden to any either to leave the place during the time of punishment, or to interfere in order to stay punishment, or in any way to move or meddle in the matter. Listen! Listen! Long live the Holy College!"

With that he descended and made his way back to the House. But Hilda ran to the Museum with the news.

"Why," said Jack, "what could happen better? In the House, no one knows what devilry of electricity and stuff they may have ready to hand. Here, in the open, we can defy them. Nothing remains but to wait until the prisoners are brought out, and then—then," he gasped, "remember what we were. Geoffrey, you wear the old uniform. Let the spirit of your old regiment fire your heart again. Ay, ay, you will do. Now, let us a drill a little and practice fighting together, shoulder to shoulder. Why, we are invincible."

Said I not that we might, if we ever regretted anything, regret that we did not lock these conspirators in the Museum before we brought out our prisoners to their death?

The great Bell of the House tolled; the People stood about in their quiet way, looking on, apparently unmoved, while the carpenters quickly hammered together a scaffold some six feet high.

Well. I confess it. The whole business was a mistake: the People were gone lower down than I had ever hoped: save for the shudder which naturally seized them on mention of the word Death, they showed no sign of concern. If, even then, I had gone forth to see how they took it, I might have reversed the order, and carried out the execution within. They wanted no lesson. Their Past, if it were once revived, would for the most part be a past of such struggling for life, and so much misery, that it was not likely they would care to revive it. Better the daily course, unchanged, unchangeable. Yet we know not. As my colleague in the House said, the memory is perhaps a thing indestructible. At a touch, at a flash of light, the whole of their minds might be lit up again; and the emotions, remembered and restored, might again seem what once they seemed, worth living for.

Still the great Bell tolled, and the carpenters hammered, and the scaffold, strong and high, stood waiting for the criminals; and on the scaffold a block, brought from the butcher's shop. But the People said not a single word to each other, waiting, like sheep—only, unlike sheep, they did not huddle together. In the chamber over the Porch the prisoners awaited the completion of the preparations; and in the Museum the fifteen conspirators stood waiting, armed and ready for their Deed of Violence.

XIII

The Execution

As the clock struck two, a messenger brought the news that the Preparations were complete.

The College was still sitting in Council. One of the Physicians proposed that before the Execution the Arch Physician should be brought before us to be subjected to a last examination. I saw no use for this measure, but I did not oppose it; and presently John Lax, armed with his sharpened axe, brought the Prisoners before the Conclave of his late brethren.

"Dr. Linister," I said, "before we start upon that Procession from which you will not return, have you any communication to make to the College? Your Researches—"

"They are all in order, properly drawn up, arranged in columns, and indexed," he replied. "I trust they will prove to advance the Cause of Science—true Science—not the degradation of Humanity."

"Such as they are, we shall use them," I replied, "according to the Wisdom of the College. Is there anything else you wish to communicate? Are there ideas in your brain which you would wish to write down before you die? Remember, in a few minutes you will be a senseless lump of clay, rolling round and round the world forever, like all the other lumps which form the crust of the Earth."

"I have nothing more to communicate. Perhaps, Suffragan, you are wrong about the senseless lumps of clay. And now, if you please, do not delay the end longer, for the sake of those poor girls waiting in suspense."

I could have wished more outward show of horror—prayers for forgiveness. No: Dr. Linister was always, in his own mind, an Aristocrat. The aristocratic spirit! How it survives even after the whole of the Past might have been supposed to be forgotten. Well: he was a tall and manly man, and he looked a born leader—a good many of them in the old days used to have that look. For my own part, I am short and black of face. No one would call me a leader born. But I deposed the Aristocrat. And as for him—what has become of him?

"What would you have done for the People?" I asked him, "that would have been better for them than forgetfulness and freedom from pain and anxiety? You have always opposed the Majority. Tell us, at this supreme moment, what you would have done for them."

"I know not now," he replied. "A month ago I should have told you that I would have revived the ancient order; I would have given the good things of the world to them who were strong enough to win them in the struggle: hard work, bad food, low condition should have been, as it used to be, the lot of the incompetent. I would have recognized in women their instinct for fine dress; I would have encouraged the revival of Love: I would have restored the Arts. But now—now—"

"Now," I said, "that you have begun to make the attempt, you recognize at last that there is nothing better for them all than forgetfulness and freedom from anxiety, struggle, and thought."

"Not so," he replied. "Not at all. I understand that unless the Spirit of Man mounts higher continually, the earthly things must grow stale and tedious, and so must perish. Yea: all the things which once we thought so beautiful—Music, Art, Letters, Philosophy, Love, Society—they must all wither and perish, if Life be prolonged, unless the Spirit is borne continually upward. And this we have not tried to effect."

"The Spirit of Man? I thought that old superstition was cleared away and done with long ago. I have never found the Spirit in my Laboratory. Have you?"

"No, I have not. That is not the place to find it."

"Well. Since you have changed your mind—"

"With us, the Spirit of Man has been sinking lower and lower, till it is clean forgotten. Man now lives for himself alone. The Triumph of Science, Suffragan, is yours. No more death; no more pain; no more ambition: equality absolute and the ultimate lump of human flesh, incorruptible, breathing, sleeping, absorbing food, living. Science can do no more."

"I am glad, even at this last moment, to receive this submission of your opinions."

"But," he said, his eye flashing, "remember. The Spirit of Man only sleeps: it doth not die. Such an awakening as you have witnessed among a few of us will some day—by an accident, by a trick of memory—how do I know? by a Dream! fly through the heads of these poor helpless sheep and turn them again into Men and Women, who will rend you. Now take me away."

It is pleasant to my self-esteem, I say, to record that one who was so great an inquirer into the Secrets of Nature should at such a moment give way and confess that I was right in my administration of the People. Pity that he should talk the old nonsense. Why, I learned to despise it in the old days when I was a boy and listened to the fiery orators of the Whitechapel Road.

The Procession was formed. It was like that of the Daily March to the Public Hall, with certain changes. One of them was that the Arch Physician now walked in the middle instead of at the end; he was no more clothed in the robes of office, but in the strange and unbecoming garb in which he was arrested. Before him walked the two women. They held a book between them, brought out of the Library by Christine, and one of them read aloud. It was, I believe, part of the incantation or fetish worship of the old time: and as they read, the tears rolled down their cheeks; yet they did not seem to be afraid.

Before the Prisoners marched John Lax, bearing the dreadful axe, which he had now polished until it was like a mirror or a laboratory tool for brightness. And on his face there still shone the honest satisfaction of one whose heart is joyed to execute punishment upon traitors. He showed this joy in a manner perhaps unseemly to the gravity of the occasion, grinning as he walked and feeling the edge of the axe with his fingers.

The way seemed long. I, for one, was anxious to get the business over and done with. I was oppressed by certain fears—or doubts—as if something would happen. Along the way on either side stood the People, ranged in order, silent, dutiful, stupid. I scanned their faces narrowly as I walked. In most there was not a gleam of intelligence. They understood nothing. Here and there a face which showed a spark of uneasiness or terror. For the most part, nothing. I began to understand that we had made a blunder in holding a Public Execution. If it was meant to impress the People, it failed to do so. That was certain, so far.

What happened immediately afterwards did, however, impress them as much as they could be impressed.

Immediately in front of the Public Hall stood the newly-erected scaffold. It was about six feet high, with a low hand-rail round it, and it was draped in black. The block stood in the middle.

It was arranged that the Executioner should first mount the scaffold alone, there to await the criminals. The College of Physicians were to sit in a semicircle of seats arranged for them on one side of it, the Bedells standing behind them; the Assistants of the College were arranged on the opposite side of the scaffold. The first to suffer was to be the girl Christine. The second, the woman Mildred. Last, the greatest criminal of the three, the Arch Physician himself.

The first part of the programme was perfectly carried out. John Lax, clothed in red, big and burly, his red face glowing, stood on the scaffold beside the block, leaning on the dreadful axe. The Sacred College were seated in their places; the Bedells stood behind them; the Assistants sat on the other side. The Prisoners stood before the College. So far all went well. Then I rose and read in a loud voice the Crimes which had been committed and the sentence of the Court. When I concluded I looked around. There was a vast sea of heads before me. In the midst I observed some kind of commotion as of people who were pushing to the front. It was in the direction of the Museum. But this I hardly noticed, my mind being full of the Example which was about to be made. As for the immobility of the People's faces, it was something truly wonderful.

"Let the woman Christine," I cried, "mount the scaffold and meet her doom!"

The girl threw herself into the arms of the other woman, and they kissed each other. Then she tore herself away, and the next moment she would have mounted the steps and knelt before the block, but. . .

The confusion which had sprung up in the direction of the Museum increased suddenly to a tumult. Right and left the people parted, flying and shrieking. And there came running through the lane thus formed a company of men, dressed in fantastic garments of various colors, armed with ancient weapons, and crying aloud, "To the Rescue! To the Rescue!"

Then I sprang to my feet, amazed. Was it possible—could it be possible—that the Holy College of Physicians should be actually defied?

It was possible; more, it was exactly what these wretched persons proposed to dare and to do.

As for what followed, it took but a moment. The men burst into the circle thus armed and thus determined. We all sprang to our feet and recoiled. But there was one who met them with equal courage and defiance. Had there been—but how could there be?—any more, we should have made a wholesome example of the Rebels.

John Lax was this one.

He leaped from the scaffold with a roar like a lion, and threw himself upon the men who advanced, swinging his heavy axe around him as if it had been a walking-stick. No wild beast deprived of its prey could have presented such a terrible appearance. Baffled revenge—rage—the thirst for battle—all showed themselves in this giant as he turned a fearless front to his enemies and swung his terrible axe.

I thought the rebels would have run. They wavered; they fell back; then at a word from their leader—it was none other than the dangerous man, the sailor called Jack, or John, Carera—they closed in and stood shoulder to shoulder, every man holding his weapon in readiness. They were armed with the ancient weapon called the rifle, with a bayonet thrust in at the end of it.

"Close in, my men; stand firm!" shouted the sailor. "Leave John Lax to me. Ho! ho! John Lax, you and I will fight this out. I know you. You were the spy who did the mischief. Come on. Stand firm, my men; and if I fall, make a speedy end of this spy and rescue the Prisoners."

He sprang to the front, and for a moment the two men confronted each other. Then John Lax, with another roar, swung his axe. Had it descended upon the sailor's head, there would have been an end of him. But—I know little of fighting; but it is certain that the fellow was a coward. For he actually leaped lightly back and dodged the blow. Then, when the axe had swung round so as to leave his adversary's side in a defenceless position, this disgraceful coward leaped forward and took a shameful advantage of this accident, and drove his bayonet up to the hilt in the unfortunate Executioner's body!

John Lax dropped his axe, threw up his arms, and fell heavily backwards. He was dead. He was killed instantaneously. Anything more terrible, more murderous, more cowardly, I never witnessed. I know, I say, little of fighting and war. But this, I must always maintain, was a foul blow. John Lax had aimed his stroke and missed, it is true, owing to the cowardly leap of his enemy out of the way. But in the name of common fairness his adversary should have permitted him to resume his fighting position. As it was, he only waited, cowardly, till the heavy axe swinging round exposed John's side, and then stepped in and took his advantage. This I call murder, and not war.

John Lax was quite dead. Our brave and zealous servant was dead. He lay on his back; there was a little pool of blood on the ground: his clothes were stained with blood: his face was already white. Was it possible? Our servant—the sacred servant of the Holy House—was dead! He had been killed! A servant of the Holy College had been killed! What next? What dreadful thing would follow? And the Criminals were rescued!

By this time we were all standing bewildered, horrified, in an undignified crowd, Fellows and Assistants together. Then I spoke, but I fear in a trembling voice.

"Men!" I said. "Know you what you do? Go back to the place whence you came, and await the punishment due to your crime. Back, I say!"

"Form in Square," ordered the murderer, paying no heed at all to my commands.

The Rebels arranged themselves—as if they had rehearsed the thing for weeks—every man with his weapon ready: five on a side, forming three sides of a square, of which the scaffold formed the fourth. Within the Square stood the three prisoners.

"O Jack!" cried Christine. "We never dreamed of this."

"O Harry!" murmured Mildred, falling into the arms of the rescued Dr. Linister. At such a moment, the first thing they thought of was this new-found love. And yet there are some who have maintained that human nature could have been continued by Science on the old lines! Folly at the bottom of everything! Folly and Vanity!

"Sir," the Sailor man addressed Dr. Linister, "you are now our Chief. Take this sword and the command."

He threw a crimson sash over the shoulders of him who but a minute before was waiting to be executed, and placed in his hands a drawn sword.

Then the Chief—I am bound to say that he looked as if he were born to command—mounted the scaffold and looked round with eyes of authority.

"Let the poor People be dismissed," he said. "Bid them disperse—go home—go to walk, and to rest or sleep, or anything that is left in the unhappy blank that we call their mind."

Then he turned to the College.

"There were some among you, my former Brethren," he said, "who in times past were friends of my own. You voted with me against the degradation of the People, but in vain. We have often communed together on the insufficiency of Science and the unwisdom of the modern methods. Come out from the College, my friends, and join us. We have the Great Secret, and we have all the knowledge of Science that there is. Cast in your lot with mine."

Five or six of the Fellows stepped forth—they were those who had always voted for the Arch Physician—among them was the man who had spoken on the uncertainty of memory. These were admitted within the line of armed men. Nay, their gowns of office were taken from them and they presently received weapons. About twenty or thirty of the Assistants also fell out and were admitted to the ranks of the Rebels.

"There come no more?" asked the Chief. "Well, choose for yourselves. Captain Heron, make the crowd stand back—clear them away with the butt ends of your rifles, if they will not go when they are told. So. Now let the rest of the College return to the House. Captain Carera, take ten men and drive them back. Let the first who stops, or endeavors to make the others stop, or attempts to address the people, be run through, as you despatched the man John Lax. Fellows and Assistants of the College—back to the place whence you came. Back, as quickly as may be, or it will be the worse for you."

The ten men stepped out with lowered bayonets. We saw them approaching with murder in their eyes, and we turned and fled. It was not a retreat: it was a helter-skelter run—one over the other. If one fell, the savage Rebels prodded him in fleshy parts and roared with laughter. Fellows, Assistants, and Bedells alike—we fell over each other, elbowing and fighting, until we found ourselves at last—some with bleeding noses, some with black eyes, some with broken ribs, all with torn gowns—within the House of Life.

The Rebels stood outside the South Porch, laughing at our discomfiture.

"Wardens of the Great Secret," said Captain Carera, "you have no longer any Secret to guard. Meantime, until the pleasure of the Chief, and the Sentence of the Court is pronounced, REMEMBER. He who endeavors to escape from the House will assuredly meet his death. Think of John Lax, and do not dare to resist the authority of the Army."

Then he shut the door upon us and locked it, and we heard the footsteps of the men as they marched away in order.

This, then, was the result of my most fatal error. Had we, as we might so easily have done, executed our prisoners in the House itself, and locked up the Rebels in the Museum, these evils would not have happened. It is futile to regret the past, which can never be undone. But it is impossible not to regret a blunder which produced such fatal results.

WALTER BESANT

XIV

Prisoners

Thus, then, were the tables turned upon us. We were locked up, prisoners—actually the Sacred College, prisoners—in the House of Life itself, and the Great Secret was probably by this time in the hands of the Rebels, to whom the Arch Traitor had no doubt given it, as he had proposed to do when we arrested him. Lost to us forever! What would become of the College when the Great Mystery was lost to it? Where would be its dignity? Where its authority?

The first question—we read it in each other's eyes without asking it—was, however, not what would become of our authority, but of ourselves. What were they going to do with us? They had killed the unfortunate John Lax solely because he stood up manfully for the College. What could we expect? Besides, we had fully intended to kill the Rebels. Now we were penned up like fowls in a coop, altogether at their mercy. Could one have believed that the Holy College, the Source of Health, the Maintainer of Life, would ever have been driven to its House, as to a prison, like a herd of swine to their sty; made to run head over heels, tumbling over one another, without dignity or self-respect; shoved, bundled, cuffed, and kicked into the House of Life, and locked up, with the promise of instant Death to any who should endeavor to escape? But did they mean to kill us? That was the Question before us. Why should they not? We should have killed the Arch Physician, had they suffered it; and now they had all the power.

I confess that the thought of this probability filled my mind with so great a terror that the more I thought of it the more my teeth chattered and my knees knocked together. Nay, the very tears—the first since I was a little boy—came into my eyes in thinking that I must abandon my Laboratory and all my Researches, almost at the very moment when the Triumph of Science was well within my grasp, and I was ready—nearly—to present Mankind at his last and best. But at this juncture the Assistants showed by their behavior and their carriage—now greatly wanting in respect—that they looked to us for aid, and I hastily called together the remaining Fellows in the Inner House.

We took our places and looked at each other in dismay which could not be concealed.

"Brothers," I said, because they looked to me for speech, "it cannot be denied that the Situation is full of Danger. Never before has the College been in danger so imminent. At this very instant they may be sending armed soldiers to murder us."

At this moment there happened to be a movement of many feet in the nave, and it seemed as if the thing was actually upon us. I sat down, pale and trembling. The others did the same. It was several minutes before confidence was so far restored that we could speak coherently.

"We have lived so long," I said, "and we have known so long the pleasure of Scientific Research, that the mere thought of Death fills us with apprehensions that the common people cannot guess. Our superior nature makes us doubly sensitive. Perhaps—let us hope—they may not kill us—perhaps they may make demands upon us to which we can yield. They will certainly turn us out of the College and House of Life and install themselves, unless we find a way to turn the tables. But we may buy our lives: we may even become their assistants. Our knowledge may be placed at their disposal—"

"Yes, yes," they all agreed. "Life before everything. We will yield to any conditions."

"The Great Secret has gone out of our keeping," I went on. "Dr. Linister has probably communicated it to all alike. There goes the whole Authority, the whole Mystery, of the College."

"We are ruined!" echoed the Fellows in dismay.

"Half a dozen of our Fellows have gone over, too. There is not now a Secret, or a Scientific Discovery, or a Process, concerning Life, Food, Health, or Disease, that they do not know as well as ourselves. And they have all the Power. What will they do with it? What can we do to get it out of their hands?"

Then began a Babel of suggestions and ideas. Unfortunately every plan proposed involved the necessity of some one risking or losing his life. In the old times, when there were always men risking and losing their lives for some cause or other, I suppose there would have been no difficulty at all. I had been accustomed to laugh at this foolish sacrifice of one's self—since there is but one life—for pay, or for the good of others. Now, however, I confess that we should have found it most convenient if we could have persuaded some to risk—very likely they would not actually have lost—their lives for the sake of the Holy

College. For instance, the first plan that occurred to us was this. We numbered, even after the late defections, two hundred strong in the College. This so-called "Army" of the Rebels could not be more than seventy, counting the deserters from the College. Why should we not break open the doors and sally forth, a hundred—two hundred—strong, armed with weapons from the laboratory, provided with bottles of nitric and sulphuric acid, and fall upon the Rebel army suddenly while they were unprepared for us?

This plan so far carried me away that I called together the whole of the College—Assistants, Bedells, and all—and laid it before them. I pointed out that the overwhelming nature of the force we could hurl upon the enemy would cause so great a terror to fall upon them that they would instantly drop their arms and fly as fast as they could run, when our men would have nothing more to do but to run after and kill them.

The men looked at one another with doubtful eyes. Finally, one impudent rascal said that as the Physicians themselves had most to lose, they should themselves lead the assault. "We will follow the Suffragan and the Fellows," he said.

I endeavored to make them understand that the most valuable lives should always be preserved until the last. But in this I failed.

The idea, therefore, of a sortie in force had to be abandoned.

It was next proposed that we should dig a tunnel under the Public Hall and blow up the Rebels with some of the old explosives. But to dig a tunnel takes time, and then who would risk his life with the explosive?

It was further proposed to send out a deputation of two or three, who should preach to the Rebels and point out the terrible consequences of their continued mutiny. But this appeared impracticable, for the simple reason that no one could be found to brave the threat of Captain Carera of death to any who ventured out. Besides, it was pointed out, with some reason, that if our messengers were suffered to reach the Rebels, no one would be moved by the threats of helpless prisoners unable to effect their own release. As for what was proposed to be done with electricity, hand-grenades, dynamite, and so forth, I pass all that over. In a word, we found that we could do nothing. We were prisoners.

Then an idea occurred to me. I remembered how, many years before, Dr. Linister, who had always a mind full of resource and ingenuity, made a discovery by means of which one man, armed with a single weapon easy to carry, could annihilate a whole army. If war had continued in the world, this weapon would have put an immediate stop to it. But war ceased, and it was never used. Now, I thought, if I could find that weapon or any account or drawing of its manufacture, I should be able from the commanding height of the Tower, with my own hand, to annihilate Dr. Linister and all his following.

I proceeded, with the assistance of the whole College, to hunt among the volumes of Researches and Experiments. There were thousands of them. We spent many days in the search. But we found it not. When we were tired of the search we would climb up into the Tower and look out upon the scene below, which was full of activity and bustle. Oh! if we could only by simply pointing the weapon, only by pressing a knob, see our enemies swiftly and suddenly overwhelmed by Death!

But we could not find that Discovery anywhere. There were whole rows of volumes which consisted of nothing but indexes. But we could not find it in any of them. And so this hope failed.

They did not kill us. Every day they opened the doors and called for men to come forth and fetch food. But they did not kill us.

Yet the danger was ever present in our minds. After a week the College resolved that, since one alone of the body knew the Great Secret, that one being the most likely to be selected for execution if there were any such step taken, it was expedient that the Secret should be revealed to the whole College. I protested, but had to obey. To part with that Secret was like parting with all my power. I was no longer invested with the sanctity of one who held that Secret: the Suffragan became a simple Fellow of the College: he was henceforth only one of those who conducted Researches into Health and Food and the like.

This suspense and imprisonment lasted for three weeks. Then the Rebels, as you shall hear, did the most wonderful and most unexpected thing in the world. Why they did it, when they had the House of Life, the College, and all in their own hands, and could have established themselves there and done whatever they pleased with the People, I have never been able to understand.

XV

The Recruiting Sergeant

When the College had thus ignominiously been driven into the House and the key turned upon us, the Rebels looked at each other with the greatest satisfaction.

"So far," said Jack, "we have succeeded beyond our greatest hopes. The Prisoners are rescued; the only man with any fight in him has been put out of the temptation to fight any more; the Holy College are made Prisoners; ourselves are masters of the field, and certain to remain so; and the People are like lambs—nothing to be feared from them—nothing, apparently, to be hoped."

They had been reduced to terror by the violence of the Rebels in pushing through them; they had rushed away, screaming: those of them who witnessed the horrible murder of John Lax were also seized with panic, and fled. But when no more terrifying things befell, they speedily relapsed into their habitual indifference, and crept back again, as if nothing had happened at all, to dawdle away their time in the sunshine and upon the garden benches—every man alone, as usual. That the Holy College were Prisoners—that Rebels had usurped the Authority—affected them not a whit, even if they understood it. My administration had been even too successful. One could no longer look to the People for anything. They were now, even more rapidly than I had thought possible, passing into the last stages of human existence.

"Ye Gods!" cried Dr. Linister, swearing in the language of the Past and by the shadows long forgotten. "Ye Gods! How stupid they have become! I knew not that they were so far gone. Can nothing move them? They have seen a victorious Rebellion—a Revolution, not without bloodshed. But they pay no heed. Will nothing move them? Will words? Call some of them together, Jack. Drive them here. Let us try to speak to them. It may be that I shall touch some chord which will recall the Past. It was thus that you—we—were all awakened from that deadly Torpor."

Being thus summoned, the People—men and women—flocked about the scaffold, now stripped of its black draperies, and listened while Dr. Linister harangued them. They were told to stand and listen, and they obeyed, without a gleam in their patient, sheep-like faces to show that they understood.

"I CAN DO NO MORE!" cried Dr. Linister, after three-quarters of an hour.

He had drawn a skilful and moving picture of the Past; he had depicted its glories and its joys, compared with the dismal realities of the Present. He dwelt upon their loveless and passionless existence; he showed them how they were gradually sinking lower and lower—that they would soon lose the intelligence necessary even for the daily task. Then he asked them if they would join his friends and himself in the new Life which they were about to begin: it should be full of all the old things—endeavor, struggle, ambition, and Love. They should be alive, not half dead.

More he said—a great deal more—but to no purpose. If they showed any intelligence at all, it was terror at the thought of change.

Dr. Linister descended.

"It is no use," he said. "Will you try, Jack?"

"Not by speaking. But I will try another plan."

He disappeared, and presently came back again, having visited the cellars behind the Public Halls. After him came servants, rolling barrels and casks at his direction.

"I am going to try the effect of a good drink," said Jack. "In the old days they were always getting drunk, and the trades had each their favorite liquor. It is now no one knows how long since these poor fellows have had to become sober, because they could no longer exceed their ration. Let us encourage them to get drunk. I am sure that ought to touch a chord."

This disgraceful idea was actually carried out. Drink of all kinds—spirits, beer, and every sort of intoxicating liquor—were brought forth, and the men were invited to sit down and drink freely, after the manner of the old time.

When they saw the casks brought out and placed on stands, each ready with its spigot, and, beside the casks, the tables and benches, spread for them—on the benches, pipes and tobacco—gleams of intelligence seemed to steal into their eyes.

"Come," said Jack, "sit down, my friends; sit down, all of you. Now then, what will you drink? What shall it be? Call for what you like best. Here is a barrel of beer; here is stout; here are gin, whiskey, rum,

Hollands, and brandy. What will you have? Call for what you please. Take your pipes. Why, it is the old time over again."

They looked at each other stupidly. The very names of these drinks had been long forgotten by them. But they presently accepted the invitation, and began to drink greedily. At seven o'clock, when the Supper Bell rang, there were at least three hundred men lying about, in various stages of drunkenness. Some were fast asleep, stretched at their full length on the ground; some lay with their heads on the table; some sat, clutching at the pewter mugs; some were vacuously laughing or noisily singing.

"What do you make of your experiment?" asked Dr. Linister. "Have you struck your chord?"

"Well, they have done once more what they used to do," said Jack, despondently; "and they have done it in the same old way. I don't think there could ever have been any real jolliness about the dogs, who got drunk as fast as ever they could. I expected a more gradual business. I thought the drink would first unloose their tongues, and set them talking. Then I hoped that they would, in this way, be led to remember the Past; and I thought that directly they began to show any recollection at all, I would knock off the supply and carry on the memory. But the experiment has failed, unless"—here a gleam of hope shone in his face—"to-morrow's hot coppers prove a sensation so unusual as to revive the memory of their last experience in the same direction—never mind how many years ago. Hot coppers *may* produce that result."

He ordered the casks to be rolled back to the cellars. That evening the Rebels, headed by Dr. Linister—all dressed in scarlet and gold, with swords—and with them the ladies—(they were called ladies now, nothing less—not women of the People any more)—came to the Public Hall, dressed for the evening in strange garments, with bracelets, necklaces, jewels, gloves, and things which most of the People had never seen. But they seemed to take no heed of these things.

"They are hopeless," said Jack. "Nothing moves them. We shall have to begin our new life with our own company of thirty."

"Leave them to us," said Mildred. "Remember, it was by dress that Christine aroused us from our stagnant condition; and it was by us that you men were first awakened. Leave them to us."

After the evening meal the ladies went about from table to table, talking to the women. Many of these, who had belonged to the working classes in the old Time, and had no recollection at all of fine dress, looked stupidly at the ladies' dainty attire. But there were others whose faces seemed to show possibilities of other things. And to these the ladies addressed themselves. First, they asked them to look at their fine frocks and bangles and things; and next, if any admiration was awakened, they begged them to take off their flat caps and to let down their hair. Some of them consented, and laughed with new-born pride in showing off their long-forgotten beauty. Then the ladies tied ribbons round their necks and waists, put flowers into their hair, and made them look in the glass. Not one of those who laughed and looked in the glass but followed the ladies that evening to the Museum.

They came—a company of Recruits fifty strong, all girls. And then the whole evening was devoted to bringing back the Past. It came quickly enough to most. To some, a sad Past, full of hard, underpaid work; to some, a Past of enforced idleness; to some, a Past of work and pay and contentment. They were shopgirls, work-girls, ballet-girls, barmaids— all kinds of girls. To every one was given a pretty and becoming dress; not one but was rejoiced at the prospect of changing the calm and quiet Present for the emotions and the struggles of the Past.

But they were not allowed to rest idle. Next day these girls again, with the ladies, went out and tried the effect of their new dress and their newly-restored beauty upon other women first, and the men afterwards. As they went about, lightly and gracefully, singing, laughing, daintily dressed, many of the men began to lift up their sleepy eyes, and to look after them. And when the girls saw these symptoms, they laid siege to such a man, two or three together; or perhaps one alone would undertake the task, if he was more than commonly susceptible. As for those on whom bright eyes, smiles, laughter, and pretty dresses produced no effect, they let them alone altogether. But still Recruits came in fast.

Every night they did all in their power to make the Past live again. They played the old Comedies, Melodramas, and Farces in the Public Hall; they sang the old songs; they encouraged the Recruits to sing; they gave the men tobacco and beer; they had dances and music. Every morning the original company of Rebels sat in Council. Every afternoon the Recruits, dressed like soldiers of the Past, were drawn up, drilled, and put through all kinds of bodily exercise.

WE WERE PRISONERS, I SAID, for three weeks.

One morning, at the end of that time, a message came to us from the "Headquarters of the Army." This was now their official style and title. The Chief ordered the immediate attendance of the Suffragan and two Fellows of the College of Physicians.

At this terrifying order, I confess that I fell into so violent a trembling—for, indeed, my last hour seemed now at hand—that I could no longer stand upright; and, in this condition of mind, I was carried—being unable to walk, and more dead than alive—out of the House of Life to the Headquarters of the Rebel Army.

XVI

A Most Unexpected Conclusion

I confess, I say, that I was borne in a half-fainting condition from the House of Life.

"Farewell, Suffragan, farewell!" said my Brethren of the College, gathered within the South Porch, where a guard of armed Rebels waited for us. "Your turn to-day, ours to-morrow! Farewell! Yet if any concessions can be made—"

Yes—yes—if any concessions could be made, only to save life, they might be certain that I should make them. The two Fellows of the College upon whom the lot—they drew lots—had fallen, accompanied me, with cheeks as pallid and hearts as full of terror as my own.

A company of twenty men, armed, escorted us. I looked on the way for lines of People to witness the Downfall of the College and the Execution of its Heads. I looked for the scaffold which we had erected, and for the executioner whom we had provided. I listened for the Great Bell which we had caused to be rung.

Strange! There were no People at all; the way from the House was quite clear; the People were engaged as usual at their work. I saw no scaffold, and no executioner. I heard no Great Bell. Yet the absence of these things did not reassure me in the least.

But everything, even in these short three weeks, was changed. Nearly the whole of the open space before the Public Hall was now covered with rows of gay-colored tents, over which flew bright little flags. They were quite small tents, meant, I learned afterwards, for sleeping. Besides these there were great tents open at the sides, and spread, within, with tables and benches, at which sat men smoking tobacco and drinking beer, though it was as yet only the forenoon. Some of them were playing cards, some were reading books, and some—a great many—were eagerly talking. They were all dressed in tunics of scarlet, green, and gray, and wore leathern belts with helmets—the costume seemed familiar to me. Then I remembered; it was the old dress of a soldier. Wonderful! After Science had lavished all her resources in order to suppress and destroy among the People the old passions—at the very first opportunity the Rebels had succeeded in awakening them again in their worst and most odious form!

There were also large open spaces upon which, regardless of the flower-beds, some of the men were marching up and down in line, carrying arms, and performing evolutions to the command of an officer.

Some of the men, again, lay sprawling about on benches, merely looking on and doing nothing—yet with a lively satisfaction in their faces. They ought to have been in the fields or the workshops. And everywhere among the men, looking on at the drill, sitting in the tents, walking beside them, sitting with them on the benches, were the girls, dressed and adorned after the bad old false style, in which the women pretended to heighten and set off what they are pleased to call their charms by garments fantastically cut, the immodest display of an arm or a neck, hair curiously dressed and adorned, colored ribbons, flowers stuck in their hats, and ornaments tied on wherever it was possible. And such joy and pride in these silly decorations! No one would believe how these girls looked at each other and themselves. But to think that the poor silly men should have fallen into the nets thus clumsily spread for them! And this, after all our demonstrations to show that woman bears in every limb the mark of inferiority, so that contempt, or at least pity, and not admiration at all, to say nothing of the extraordinary foolish passion of Love, should be the feeling of man for woman! However, at this moment I was naturally too much occupied with my own danger to think of these things.

One thing, however, one could not avoid remarking. The Rebellion must have spread with astonishing rapidity. It was no longer a company of fifteen or sixteen men—it was a great Army that we saw. And there was no longer any doubt possible as to the movement. The Past was restored. In the faces of the young men and the girls, as we passed through them, I remarked, sick with terror as I was, the old, old expression which I hoped we had abolished forever—the eagerness, the unsatisfied desire, and the Individualism. Yes—the Individualism. I saw on their faces, plain to read, the newly-restored Rights of Property.

Why, as I walked through one of the groups, composed of men and women, one of the men suddenly rushed forward and struck another in the face with his fist.

"She's my girl!" he cried, hoarsely. "Touch her if you dare."

They closed round the pair and led them off.

"Going to fight it out," said one of our Guards.

To fight it out! What a Fall! To fight it out!—To call a woman—or anything else—your own after all our teaching. And to fight it out! And all this arrived at in three weeks!

These things I observed, I say, as one observes things in a dream, and remembers afterwards.

My heart failed me altogether, and I nearly fainted, when we stopped at a long tent before which floated a flag on a flagstaff.

They carried me within and placed me in a chair. As soon as my eyes recovered the power of sight I saw, sitting at the head of the table, Dr. Linister, dressed in some sort of scarlet coat, with a sash and gold lace. Then, indeed, I gave myself up for lost. It was the Court, and we were called before it to receive sentence. At his side sat half a dozen officers bravely dressed. The tent was filled with others, including many women richly dressed—I observed the woman Mildred, clad in crimson velvet, and the girl Christine, in white, and I thought they regarded me with vindictive eyes.

When we were seated, Dr. Linister looked up—his face was always grave, but it was no longer melancholy. There was in it, now, something of Hope or Triumph or Resolution—I know not what.

"Brothers," he said, gravely, "once my brothers of the College, I have called you before us in order to make a communication of the greatest importance, and one which will doubtless cause you considerable surprise. What is the matter, Suffragan? Hold him up, somebody. We desire that you should hear from our own lips what we propose to do.

"First, will somebody give Dr. Grout a glass of wine or brandy, or something? Pray be reassured, gentlemen. No harm, I promise, shall happen to any of you. First, in a day or two the doors of the House will be thrown open, and you shall be free again to renew your old life—if you still feel disposed to do so. I repeat that no violence is intended towards you. Grout, pull yourself together, man. Sit up, and leave off shaking. You will be able without opposition, I say, to carry on again your Administration of the People on the old lines. I trust, however, that you will consider the situation, and the condition to which you have reduced unfortunate Humanity, very seriously.

"In short, though we are absolute masters of the situation, and now command a Force against which it would be absurd for you to contend, we are going to abandon the Field, and leave everything to you." Were we dreaming? "The Present is so odious to our People; the surroundings of this place are so full of the horrible and loathsome Present, that we have resolved to leave it altogether. We find, in fact, that it will be impossible to begin the new Life until all traces of your Administration are removed or lost. And we shall be so much clogged by your Public Halls, your houses, your system, and the miserable lives to which you have reduced most of the men and women, that we must either send them—and you—away, or go away ourselves. On the whole, it will give us less trouble to go away ourselves. Therefore, as soon as our Preparations are ready, we shall go.

"We shall carry with us from the Common Stores all that we shall be likely to want in starting our New Community. We shall leave you to work out, undisturbed, the Triumph of Science, as you understand it, upon these poor wretches, already more than half stupefied by your treatment.

"We shall take with us all those whom by any means—by the beauty of women, the splendor of arms, the ancient dresses, the ancient music, the ancient dances—we have been able to awaken from their torpor. They amount in all to no more than a thousand or so of young men and as many maidens. As for the rest, they are sunk in a lethargy so deep that we have been unable to rouse them. They are already very near to the condition which you desire.

"Yet I know not. These poor dull brains may be swiftly and suddenly fired with some contagion which may at any time ruin your calculations and destroy the boasted Triumph. Do not rely too much upon the Torpor of this apparently helpless herd. You had at the beginning a grand weapon with which to enslave them. You could keep them alive, and you could save them from disease—if only they were obedient. If they once get beyond the recollection or the fear of either, what will you do?

"We go"—he paused, and looked round the room, filled with the eager faces which brought the Past back to me—futile eagerness! ever pressing on, gaining nothing, sinking into the grave before there was time to gain anything! That had come back—that! "We go," he repeated—his face had long been so melancholy that one hardly knew him for the same man, so triumphant was it now—"we go to repair the mistakes of many, many years. We go to lead Mankind back into the ancient paths. It was not altogether you, my friends, who destroyed Humanity; it was mainly the unfortunate Discovery of the German Professor. We were working admirably in the right direction; we were making life longer, which was then far too short; we were gradually preventing diseases, which had been beyond the control of our wisest men; we were, by slow degrees, in the only true way—through the Revelation of Nature—feeling our way to Health and Prolongation of Life. Yet, whatever happened, whatever we might discover, the First

Law of Life—which we did not understand—was that to all things earthly there must come an End.

"Then happened the event by which that End was indefinitely postponed.

"Again, I say, I blame not you so much as the current of events which bore you along. It seemed logical that everybody, able or imbecile, weak or strong, healthy or sickly, skilled or incompetent, should alike reap the Fruits of the Great Discovery. If he did so, he was also entitled to his equal share in the world's goods. This was the Right of Man, put forward as if there could be no question at all about it. Every child was to inherit an equal share of everything. It was a false and a mischievous claim. What every child inherited was the right of fighting for his share, without danger of injustice or oppression. And the next step, after the Slaughter of the Old, was the forbidding of more births. What that has done for the world, look round and see for yourselves in the torpor of the women and the apathy of the men.

"The People by this time had learned the great lesson that you wished to teach them—that Death and Disease were the only two evils. Then the College of Physicians took the place of the former Priesthood, with its own Mysteries to guard and its gifts to distribute. I do not deny that you—we—have done the work well. The Prevention of the old Diseases is nearly perfect. Yet, at any moment, a new class of Disease may spring up and baffle all your Science."

He had often talked in this way before, but never with so much authority. Yet he was going to abandon the whole—all that he and his friends had gained! Were we dreaming? His talk about my Administration affected me not one whit. I knew all his arguments. But the thought that he was going away, that he would actually leave us in Power and Possession, filled me with amazement.

The others looked and listened as if he were speaking for them.

"The Right of Man to an equal share in everything has been carried out. Look around you, and ask yourselves if the result is satisfactory. I have often asked you that question. You have replied that the Present is only a stage in the Triumph of Science. What is the next stage? To that question also you have a reply.

"Well, we give it back to you—the whole of your Present; your People, so stupid, so docile, so sluggish; your House; your College; your Secrecy; your Mystery; your Authority. Take them. You shall have them again, to do with them as seems fit to you."

At these words my heart welled over with joy. Would he really—but on what conditions?—would he really give us back the whole?

There were no conditions. He meant exactly what he said. He would give everything back to us. Were we dreaming? Were we dreaming?

"As for me and my friends," he said, "we shall sally forth to found a new Settlement, and to govern it by the ideas of the Past. No one in our Settlement will be obliged to work; but if he does not, he shall certainly starve. Nobody will inherit any share to anything except what he may win by struggle. There will be no equality at all, but every man shall have what he can honestly get for himself. No women shall be compelled to work; but they may work if they please, and at such things as they please. Many old and long-forgotten things have been already revived; such as Love: we are in love again—we, who actually forgot what love was like for all the years which we have ceased to number or to chronicle. It is impossible to describe to you, my former Brother Suffragan, who never even in the old days felt the passion—the intense joy, the ecstasy—of Love." The other men murmured approval. "But Love is a plant which, while it is hardy to endure many things, withers and dies under certain conditions. It was found to flourish in the old time, through all the changes of life: it survived the time of youth and beauty; it lasted through middle age; flourished through the scenes of old age; it lasted beyond the grave. It endured changes of fortune, decay of health, poverty, sickness, and even helplessness. But one thing kills Love. It cannot endure the dull monotony which has followed the Great Discovery: it cannot live long while the face and form know no change; while the voice never changes; while the dress, the hours of work, the work itself, the food, know no change. These are things which kill the Flower of Love. Now, all things desirable—this is a saying too hard for you, Suffragan—depend upon Love. With Love, they have revived: the courtesy of man to woman; the deference of the stronger to the weaker; the stimulus of work; hope and ambition; self-sacrifice; unselfishness; devotion; the sweet illusions of imagination—all these things have been born again within the last three weeks. They have been born again, and, with them, the necessity of an End. All things earthly most have an end." The Chief looked round him: the men murmured approval, and tears stood in the eyes of the women. "We cannot let them die. And since the First Law of Love is change—and the Certain End—we have resolved, Suffragan, on forgetting the Grand Discovery." Could this be our late Arch Physician? Were we dreaming? "We shall forego any share in it. Only the chiefs here gathered together know as yet what has been resolved. Little by little the truth will get possession of our people that an End is ordained."

We made no reply to this extraordinary announcement. What could we say? We only gasped with wonder.

"You cannot understand this, Grout. I do not expect that you should. For long years past I have understood that the Great Discovery was the greatest misfortune that ever happened to mankind. For all things must have an End: else all that is worth preserving will wither and die.

"I have nearly done. You can go back to your House, and you can carry on your Administration as you please. But there is a warning which we have first to pronounce before we let you go. Your Ultimate Triumph of Science is too great a degradation of Humanity to be endured. In years to come when our successors rule in our place, they shall send an army here to inquire into the conduct of your Trust. If we find the People more brutish, deeper sunk in apathy and torpor, that army will seize the House of Life and the College of Physicians, and will destroy your laboratories, and will suffer all—men and women of the People and Fellows of the Sacred College alike—to die. Never forget this warning. You shall surely die.

"One more point, and I have done. I mention it with diffidence, Grout, because I cannot hope for your sympathy. Your own convictions on the subject were arrived at—you have often told us—when you were a boy, and were based upon the arguments of a Sunday-morning Spouter in the Whitechapel Road. I believe that John Lax, deceased, was the Learned Authority who convinced you. Therefore, you will not understand me, Grout, when I tell you that we have found the Soul again—the long-lost Soul. All earthly things must have an End. But there are things beyond that end. Most astonishing things are likely to follow from this discovery. Long thoughts and great hopes have already begun to spring up in our minds. Our people are reading again—the old Literature is full of the Soul: they are reading the great Poets of old, and are beginning to understand what they mean. I cannot make this intelligible to you, Grout. You will not understand all that this discovery brings with it. You will never, never understand that it is a Discovery ten times—a million times—greater and better for mankind than the Great Discovery itself, of which you and I alone held the Secret.

"I take that Secret with me because I cannot forget it. But, I repeat, we shall never use it. Soon, very soon, the new active life will make men once more familiar with the old figure who carried a scythe. There will be accidents; new diseases will arise; age will creep slowly on—the Great Discovery will be quietly forgotten in minds which you had made so dull that they could not understand when we rescued them what it meant. But we, the leaders, shall know well that their happiness must have an End. All earthly things," he repeated, for the fifth time, "must have an End. That is all, Grout; but when you hear from me again, unless the Administration is changed indeed, the People—the College—and you, my Suffragan—shall all die together. You shall die, Grout! You and your friends shall die! And so, Farewell. Guard. Take them back to the House."

We returned to the House relieved of our terror, but much amazed. I had heard, in the old days, how men would be so blockishly possessed by the thought of a woman—a creature inferior to man—that they would throw away everything in the world for her sake. And now Dr. Linister himself—with all those who followed after him—had given up everything; because if Life goes, what is there left? And for the sake of a woman? What could it mean? How to explain this madness on any scientific theory? We told our Colleagues, and they marvelled; and some suspected a trick. But Dr. Linister was not a man to play tricks. As for the Soul and all that rubbish, if Dr. Linister was so mad as to give up everything for a woman, he might just as well adopt all the old Creeds together. That was no concern of ours. And as for this precious discovery about things earthly coming to an end, what had that to do with the calm and tranquil state of pure existence which we were providing for mankind? Why should that ever have an end?

THAT THREATENED ARMY HAS NEVER come. For some time the thought of it gave us considerable uneasiness. But it has never come; and I believe, for my own part, that now it never will come. As for the People, there has been no such outbreak of Memory as was prophesied. On the contrary, they have approached more and more, in docility, meekness, mindlessness, and absence of purpose, to the magnificent Ideal which I cherish for them. I know not when it will arrive; but the time is as certain to come as the morrow's sun is to dawn, when the last stage of Humanity will be reached—an inert mass of breathing, feeding, sleeping flesh, kept by the Holy College—the Triumph of Science—free from Decay and Death.

They went away in the afternoon, three or four days later. They took with them everything from the Public Stores which they thought would be useful: provisions of all kinds; wine, beer, and cider in casks; stuff for clothing; furniture; everything that they could think of. They took the pictures out of the Gallery, the books from the Library, and nearly everything that was in the Museum. From the laboratory in the House they took a great number of volumes and a quantity of instruments. At the last moment, nearly all the Assistants and the workmen agreed to join them; so that we were left with numbers greatly reduced. It is impossible to enumerate the vast quantities of things which they took with them. The wagons in which they were packed covered a couple of miles of road: the drivers were taken from the People, and ordered to discharge their duty; and, as they never came back, these poor wretches probably perished with the Rebels. They went forth in perfect order: first, an advance guard of mounted men; then a portion of the main body, among whom rode the Chief with his staff. After them came the women, some riding on horseback, among whom were the woman Mildred and the girl Christine, showing in their faces that foolish and excited happiness which is so different from the sweet tranquillity which we have introduced. Indeed, all the women were beyond themselves with this silly happiness. They sang, they laughed, they talked. Some sat in carriages of all kinds, some in wagons; some walked; and, what with their chatter and their dresses, one would have thought them a company of monkeys dressed up. After the women came the wagons, and, lastly, the rest of the men. I forgot to say that they had bands of music with them—drums, fifes, cornets, and all kinds of musical instruments—and that they carried flags, and that the men sang as they marched.

Whither they went, or what became of them—whether they carried out the desperate resolve of giving up the Great Discovery—I know not. They marched away, and we returned to our former life.

ONE THING MORE I MUST relate.

We—that is, the College—were seated, reassured as to our safety, watching this great Departure.

Five minutes or so after the women had passed, I observed two of my own friends—learned Fellows of the College, who had always followed my lead and voted with me—eagerly whispering each other, and plucking one another by the sleeve. Then they suddenly rose and pulled off their black gowns, and fled swiftly in the direction of the wagons and carriages where the women sat.

We have never seen or heard from any of these unfortunate men since.

I AM NOW MYSELF THE Arch Physician.

THE END

A Note About the Author

Walter Besant (1836–1901) was born in Portsmouth, Hampshire and studied at King's College, London. He would later work in higher education at Royal College, Mauritius, where he taught mathematics. During this time, Besant also began his extensive writing career. In 1868 he published *Studies in Early French Poetry* followed by a fruitful collaboration with James Rice, which produced *Ready-money Mortiboy* (1872), and *The Golden Butterfly* (1876). Besant's career spanned genres and mediums including fiction, non-fiction, plays and various collections.

A Note from the Publisher

Spanning many genres, from non-fiction essays to literature classics to children's books and lyric poetry, Mint Edition books showcase the master works of our time in a modern new package. The text is freshly typeset, is clean and easy to read, and features a new note about the author in each volume. Many books also include exclusive new introductory material. Every book boasts a striking new cover, which makes it as appropriate for collecting as it is for gift giving. Mint Edition books are only printed when a reader orders them, so natural resources are not wasted. We're proud that our books are never manufactured in excess and exist only in the exact quantity they need to be read and enjoyed.

bookfinity™

Discover more of your favorite classics with Bookfinity™.

- Track your reading with custom book lists.
- Get great book recommendations for your personalized Reader Type.
- Add reviews for your favorite books.
- AND MUCH MORE!

Visit **bookfinity.com** and take the fun Reader Type quiz to get started.

Enjoy our classic and modern companion pairings!

Printed in the USA
CPSIA information can be obtained
at www.ICGtesting.com
JSHW082350140824
68134JS00020B/2003

9 781513 281353